W9-BGB-270

OTHER YEARLING BOOKS YOU WILL ENJOY:

HOW TO EAT FRIED WORMS, *Thomas Rockwell*
HOW TO FIGHT A GIRL, *Thomas Rockwell*
HOW TO GET FABULOUSLY RICH, *Thomas Rockwell*
NEVER TRUST A SISTER OVER TWELVE, *Stephen Roos*
SOUP, *Robert Newton Peck*
CHOCOLATE FEVER, *Robert Kimmel Smith*
JELLY BELLY, *Robert Kimmel Smith*
MOSTLY MICHAEL, *Robert Kimmel Smith*
BOBBY BASEBALL, *Robert Kimmel Smith*
THE WAR WITH GRANDPA, *Robert Kimmel Smith*

YEARLING BOOKS are designed especially to entertain and enlighten young people. Patricia Reilly Giff, consultant to this series, received her bachelor's degree from Marymount College and a master's degree in history from St. John's University. She holds a Professional Diploma in Reading and a Doctorate of Humane Letters from Hofstra University. She was a teacher and reading consultant for many years, and is the author of numerous books for young readers.

For a complete listing of all Yearling titles, write to
Dell Readers Service,
P.O. Box 1045,
South Holland, IL 60473.

# Fig Pudding

## by Ralph Fletcher

A YEARLING BOOK

Published by
Bantam Doubleday Dell Books for Young Readers
a division of
Bantam Doubleday Dell Publishing Group, Inc.
1540 Broadway
New York, New York 10036

ISBN: 0-440-41203-X

Reprinted by arrangement with Houghton Mifflin Company

Printed in the United States of America

October 1996

10  9  8  7  6  5  4  3  2  1

OPM

I dedicate this book
to my remarkable mother
Jean Fletcher

and to Bob,

in memory

# Contents

# 1. Clifford
# Allyn Abernathy III

My full name is Clifford Allyn Abernathy III, after my father and grandfather, but I leave off the III, the *Allyn*, and the *ord*. Call me Cliff. I'm in Mr. Beck's class at the Bradford Bridges Elementary School in Ballingsford. I've noticed lately that lots of my favorite things seem to start with "B": baseball (Baltimore is my favorite team), basketball, bacon, bluefishing, blue slush cones. Brad.

I'm the oldest of six kids. And that makes me different from the other kids. Dad and Mom sure treat me different. The other kids can whoop and scream and holler like a bunch of savages. They can sneak into Mrs. Montgomery's vegetable garden and pick all her cherry tomatoes—no big deal. They can climb trees and get sticky pine pitch smeared all over their shirts and hair—what do you expect?

Dad and Mom expect more from me. I have to be

Mr. Responsibility, Mr. Set-a-Good-Example. On certain days keeping the other kids out of trouble makes me feel more like a policeman than a brother. Some days it drives me nuts.

Take the time when a water pipe burst down the street and made a huge mud puddle on the McIlreavys' front lawn. Before I could say Baby Beluga the other kids had kicked off their shoes (Teddy kept his socks on) and waded deep into the mud-brown water. I stood at the edge yelling at them to get out, secretly wishing I could go in. When we got home it didn't matter to Mom that my own clothes didn't have a speck of mud on them. She took one look at the other kids, sat me down as if it was my fault, and demanded, "How could you let this happen?"

Don't get me wrong, being the oldest has its advantages. I don't have to wear a baseball glove somebody else stunk up with years of their old sweat. I don't have any Monster Big Brother or Evil Big Sister to boss me around. I get to stay up later than anyone else. And I get to hear lots of grown-up stuff the younger kids never hear, like about why Uncle Ray doesn't come to visit anymore (he's drinking again).

"Being the oldest is special," Mom is forever saying. But when you balance out the advantages with having to act like Mr. Almost-Perfect and all the rest, take it from me, being the oldest is not all it's cracked up to be.

Living in a family with so many people can be pretty weird, too. Ever go to bed on a cold winter night with the heat turned down and your room so cold you have to pile a bunch of blankets on top of you? While you lie there you mostly feel the flannel sheet and quilt right next to you. With the other blankets, the ones added last, your body doesn't notice whether those blankets are made of wool or cotton. All you know is that they're helping keep you warm.

In a crazy way it feels like that, living in a family with so many kids: Nate, Cyn (short for Cynthia), Teddy, Brad, Josh. Nate is like my closest blanket. We're less than a year apart. We share a bedroom. The other kids are my sister and brothers, but Nate is my best friend. And then there's the baby, Josh. I was almost ten when he was born. He's okay, as babies go, but most of the time I don't pay all that much attention to him. He's like that last blanket piled on my bed just before I fall asleep.

"We Abernathys always overdo everything," Mom likes to say. True enough. I hate going with Mom to the supermarket—it's embarrassing. We end up with two shopping carts overflowing with food. Mom buys the jumbo size of everything. When she cooks, she always doubles the recipe, but after supper it's a miracle if there's any food left on the table.

We Abernathys always overdo everything, but even for us this past year has been like nothing I'd ever thought possible. Like five years crammed into one. With plenty of stuff I want to remember forever. And stuff I wish I could forget.

I only know one way to start telling about a year like this: take a deep breath, begin at the beginning, and push right on through until the end.

# 2. A Yidda Yadda

It started a few days before Christmas. I was sitting in the kitchen, getting ready to dig into a steaming plate of French toast Mom had just handed me, when she asked: "Would you cut up Josh's French toast first?"

"C'mon, Mom, I'm *starved*!" I told her.

"It'll just take a minute," she said. "I don't have four arms."

"Oh, all right," I grumbled. Josh wasn't quite two. I cut a piece of French toast, and he popped it into his mouth. I cut another, and he gobbled down that piece, too.

"Don't just swallow it," I told him. "You gotta chew or you'll get a bellyache."

Josh started coughing hard. He had a bad cold: two fat jets of greenish snot were slowly making their way down his face from nose to mouth. He grinned up, but I tried not to look at him—it was too disgusting. Finally I got his toast cut up and his nose wiped, and had just drowned my own French toast in syrup when all of a sudden I heard something at the front door.

"Watch your step, Grandma," a voice said. Dad! Grandma! A mad scramble for the front door. I jumped up first, but Teddy swerved in front of me, nearly knocked me over, and made it to the front door ahead of everyone else.

"GRANDMA!" he screamed.

Grandma Annie stood there waiting for us, a little stooped over, holding a small shopping bag. Dad stood behind her carrying two suitcases. "Grandma! Grandma!"

All six kids wrapped Grandma in a big bear hug. "Grandma! Grandma!"

"Well, hullo! Hullo!" she cried. Her face was lit up, blue eyes sparkling behind her glasses. "Hullo! Look at you all! Just look at you! How tall you all are! Cliff, you've grown half a foot since last summer!"

"Just broke five feet," I told her. I was the second-tallest kid in my class, three inches behind Melody Swift, a dorky blond-haired girl who had just moved from Tallahassee.

"Can't keep food in the refrigerator," Mom said.

"Just as it should be," Grandma told Mom. "Better to spend your money on food than on doctors' bills."

"I'm getting big, too!" Brad put in.

"Yeah, but I'm BIGGER!" Teddy yelled.

"You're all simply enormous!" Grandma said, tousling their hair.

Josh tried to climb her leg like a squirrel. She reached down and picked him up. "Well, hello there, little monkey! Just look at that runny nose! That's quite a cold you've got, young man."

"He's been sick all week," Mom sighed.

"Sick," Josh said.

"I'll make some chicken soup," Grandma said. She reached down and touched Cyn on the back of her neck. "And how are you, darling?"

"I'm good."

"Santa Claus going to bring you a special present this year?" Grandma asked her.

"PRESENTS! PRESENTS!" Teddy yelled. Mom shushed him.

"I wish he'd bring me a little sister," Cyn said quietly.

"I know, I know." Grandma stroked her cheek.

"Five brothers," Cyn said. "And me."

"It must take a mountain of patience," Grandma said.

"Buttuh goo," Josh said. Everyone laughed, but Grandma looked confused.

"He's saying: butter good," Nate explained. "Josh loves butter, don't you? Hey, Josh! Tell Grandma what you want Santa Claus to bring you."

"A yidda yadda," Josh said seriously. He sniffled and tried to wipe his runny nose, but only smeared the stuff all over his face.

"Here," Grandma Annie said, wiping his face with a tissue. "Now what did you say?"

"I wanna yidda yadda," Josh said. Grandma looked confused again.

"What's that?" she asked.

"That's the thing—no one knows," I told her. "It's a mystery. Everybody's trying to figure it out."

"Hey, Cyn, you speak baby talk, don't you?" Nate asked. "What's he saying?"

"Very funny," Cyn replied. She shrugged. "It could be almost anything. Sounds a little like *yellow water*. Or maybe *little spider*."

Grandma asked Josh, "Do you want yellow water?" He shook his head.

"Do you want a little spider?"

"No."

"Can you use some other words to tell us what you want?"

"I wanna yidda yadda," Josh repeated patiently. Then he pinched a fold of Grandma's loose neck skin and sort of stretched it out from her neck, let go, and pulled the skin out again, all the while grinning and saying, "Squishy, squishy, squishy . . ."

"Josh!" Mom said. She looked horrified.

"Oh, now that's all right." Grandma was laughing. "Guess I am pretty squishy in certain places." She grabbed a hunk of Josh's cheek. "Squishy, squishy yourself!"

Dad sent me outside to fetch the rest of Grandma's stuff. I gobbled down my French toast,

"Fat. The birds need extra fat when it's this cold. We've got to keep feeding them or they'll freeze."

"You won't start baking without us, will you?" I asked. It just killed me that Grandma Annie was visiting but I still had to go to school. It wasn't fair.

"Heavens, no!" Grandma retorted. "How could I? I've got a ton of baking—I'm going to need all the helpers I can get."

"Can I come to the store with you?" Cyn asked. "Please?"

"You have to go to school, young lady," Mom said. "You all do. Look at the clock. Get a move on! The bus will be here in five minutes."

"But I want to go shopping with Grandma!"

"I'm not going shopping," Grandma said. "Your father said he'd be nice enough to go shopping for me. I'm going to take off my shoes and put these old feet up. All this travel and excitement has worn me out!"

We went off to school. I was in fifth grade, Nate in fourth, Cyn in third, Teddy in second, Brad in first. I sat next to Nate on the bus and the whole way I thought about Grandma.

Grandma Annie needed plenty of rest because she was really old: seventy-nine years old. When she was eighteen she got a job working at Filene's department store in Boston; she played on the Filene's women's basketball team. Now she had a slow and stooped-over kind of walk, and I couldn't imagine her dribbling or shooting or guarding another player. But she had been one of the best players on the team. Dad showed me an old newspaper clipping that said, "Anne Sullivan plays the toughest defense in the league."

Back in the 1920s only men could vote—no women allowed. Grandma had marched on the Boston Common with thousands of other women who were mad about that. They wanted women to have the same right to vote. Grandma was proud: she had helped to change that law.

Annie Sullivan got married and had eight children; Mom was the youngest. Annie's husband, James, had died on Mom's thirteenth birthday. "My mother has always had a backbone like a rod of Bethlehem steel," Mom liked to say about Grandma. I guess she needed that strong backbone being a widow when her four sons (my uncles) went overseas to fight in World War II.

Now Grandma Annie lived alone. She had lots of people who loved her, tons of relatives begging her to spend the holiday with them. I always thought it was amazing, almost a miracle, that most years she chose to come to our house.

I came home from school in a bad mood. Mr. Beck's nickname was "The Bomber" because he liked to drop tons of homework at the last minute. Well, today he'd lived up to his nickname. Here it was one day before Christmas vacation and he gave us eight pages of math, two chapters in science, plus a page of homonyms and antonyms. "They'll be fun," he promised. Ha! I lugged my backpack into the kitchen. There was someone sitting at our table.

"Uncle Billy!" I cried.

"Silly Billy!" Nate yelled. He raced over and practically jumped on the man.

"Pick on someone your own size!" Uncle Billy said, pretending to be scared. "Look at the lot of you!"

"Hi, hi, hi," Brad said, jumping up on his lap. Uncle Billy was about fifty, with big shoulders and a big bald head. Brad rubbed the bald top of Uncle Billy's head and grinned. "What happened to your hair?"

"Sold it to an Englishman for a million dollars," he said.

"Really?" Brad asked, serious. Brad was the most gullible person on the planet—he believed anything. If you told him you had a stegosaurus chained up in the backyard, his first reaction would be, "Does he bite?"

"You did not sell it," Cyn said, smiling.

"I did, I did, cross my heart and hope to die!"

Uncle Billy could imitate birdcalls, tell jokes, and speak Spanish as well as Arabic and Swahili. He'd learned those languages during his twenty years in the navy. He could do dozens of amazing card tricks and just as many tricks with his hands, including one where you clearly counted eleven fingers and thumbs. Uncle Billy never explained his tricks; he never gave away his secrets. He'd fought in World War II and in the Korean War, too. Nate was forever trying to get him to tell us war stories, but what I loved most was hearing him talk about the old base-ball players: Ted Williams, Jimmy Foxx, the great DiMaggio brothers, Joe and Dom. He liked to sing:

> "He's better than his brother Joe
> Dominic DiMaggio . . . "

"So what do you ragamuffins want for Christmas this year?" Uncle Billy asked. "Cliff?"

"He wants a choo-choo train," Nate sneered.

"So what?" I shot back. I cleared my throat. "Yeah, well, I think I might start collecting Lionel train pieces. You know, as a hobby."

I was eleven years old, and part of me wondered if I wasn't too old for a train set. But I did want it something fierce. I'd seen it in a store, a Lionel train with a bright light in the front of the engine as it thundered around the track, and real smoke, oily and metallic, spilling out the top. If I started think-ing about it in bed, I'd get so excited I couldn't fall sleep.

"Aha. How about you, Nate?"

"A microscope," he said. "Or a chemistry set."

"The mad scientist." Cyn giggled.

"Watch out," Nate said, "or I'll blow up your room."

"You'll blow up yourself first," Cyn replied.

"Easy there," Uncle Billy said. "How about you, Cynthia?"

"A kitten," she said.

"Don't hold your breath," I snorted. "Haven't you heard? Dad hates cats. He's allergic."

"Is not!"

"He's allergic to the *idea* of having a cat," I said.

"Dad told me to put it on my list," Cyn said, raising her nose at me. "I also want a transistor radio."

"Rock'em Sock'em Robots!" Teddy yelled. "And boxing gloves! And a road racing set! And walkie-talkies! And—"

"His list is two pages long," Cyn told Uncle Billy. "Mom already said no to the boxing gloves."

"Did NOT!" Teddy yelled.

"Easy there, Ted," Uncle Billy said. "How about you, Brad?"

"I want a baseball glove."

"Atta boy!" Uncle Billy punched him lightly on the arm.

"I wanna yidda yadda," Josh said quietly.

"And what in tarnation is that?" Uncle Billy asked.

"That's just it," I said. "We can't find anybody who knows what a yidda yadda is."

"Sarsaparilla succotash," Uncle Billy said, snapping his fingers twice. "You know what, I think I just may have an idea. I believe that a yidda yadda is a kind of talking parrot, nearly extinct, found on the tiny island of Maskoogat just off the southernmost tip of Madagascar."

"Uncle Billy!" Cyn frowned at him. "You're being silly!"

"Well, I have read that the people of Katmandu call a yo-yo a yidda yadda," he said. "It's a kind of yo-yo that makes a strange music when you—"

"Uncle Billy!" Cyn warned. "I'm gonna tell Grandma on you!"

"Where is Grandma?" Brad asked.

"Upstairs taking a nap," Uncle Billy said. "She said you can go wake her when you get home."

"That's the first true thing you've said," Cyn told him.

Everyone started racing upstairs.

"Up! Up!" Josh said, lifting his arms to me. I lifted him and started carrying him up the stairs.

"I wanna yidda yadda," Josh whispered.

"I know, I know. But what is a yidda yadda?"

He turned to look at me. His eyes were all watery. His nose was running real bad—little faucets of greenish goop.

"A yidda yadda," Josh said, as if that explained everything.

A mystery.


"All right, everybody wake up and die right!"

Grandma said when she came down to the kitchen.

"I'm ready!" Teddy cried.

"We're making stollen," Grandma announced. "Everybody with me? Cliff?"

Grandma took my right hand in hers and gave it a squeeze. Her hands were amazing. One time when she fell asleep on the couch I spent about fifteen minutes studying her hands, the dark veins slowly throbbing under skin that looked thin and clear as tissue paper. Her hands made me think of driftwood, old and pale and worn smooth. They were stained brown in places but she still she had one strong grip.

"I'm doing the flour, right?" I asked. Whenever Grandma made stollen it was my job to sift the flour—seven cups plus a teaspoon of salt. Sifting flour made my hands ache, but it had to be done just right. I felt kind of proud knowing that Grandma trusted me to do it.

"Right! Sift that flour good—I want it light and fluffy. Teddy?"

"I'm doing the yeast!" Teddy cried.

"No, you're not!" Nate shot back. "I*m* mixing the yeast."

"THAT'S NOT FAIR!" Teddy screamed. "HE ALWAYS GETS TO DO THE YEAST!"

"Right, that's my job," Nate said.

"Here," Grandma said, giving Teddy a box of raisins. "I need you to count out fifty raisins. Put them in this bowl. Fifty. One raisin for every state in the country."

"He can't count that high," Nate muttered.

"CAN TOO!" Teddy yelled.

"Never mind about the raisins," Grandma told Nate. "You pay attention to that yeast. Remember, the water has to be *warm*. Not too hot, not too cold."

Cyn was using a hand beater to beat an egg.

"Whip that egg up nice and smooth," Grandma said.

"What're you doing, Grandma?" Cyn asked.

"Scalding this milk and keeping an eye on the rest of you!"

"Me too!" Josh pulled on Grandma's apron.

"All right!" Grandma said. "How else are we going to get these walnuts chopped up?"

She gave Josh a pile of walnuts and a block of wood for breaking the nuts into smaller pieces. That was a tradition: whenever Grandma made stollen the youngest kid always got to smash up the walnuts. Josh took the wood and started pounding like a madman, as if he wanted to pulverize each walnut right down to dust.

When we finished making the dough Grandma put it in a big bowl, covered it with a towel, and put it on the stove. It would take an hour for the dough to rise. Teddy, Brad, and Cyn dragged Grandma into the living room and pushed her back onto the couch. Brad climbed onto her lap.

"Story! Story!" they yelled. "Tell us a story, Grandma!"

"All right, all right," Grandma said. "Cliff, Nate,

you boys come over here. Don't tell me you're too old for one of your grandma's stories because I know you're not! I ever tell you about the first time I went on a vacation? You know I didn't get a vacation until I was forty-one years old!"

"How come?" I asked.

"We couldn't afford it when I was younger. We had to spend every cent we had on rent and food."

"Were you poor, Grandma?" Cyn asked.

"I don't know," she said. She stopped and seemed to think about it. "Maybe a little. Being poor is nothing to be ashamed of. We had food, we had clothes, we had beds to sleep in. We just didn't have anything left over for vacations and such. But on my forty-first birthday my brother Paul took me out to Arizona, to the desert. One morning we were driving through some little town, and all of a sudden a policeman stopped the traffic in both directions. At first we couldn't see why he was stopping us, so we got out of the car to find out what the problem was. You'll never believe what we saw."

"What?"

"We saw a family of tarantulas crossing the road! Long as I live, I'll never forget the sight of that big policeman with a whistle in his mouth holding up both hands so those tarantulas could make it safely across."

"Aw c'mon, Grandma," Nate said. He grinned and gave her a skeptical look.

"You don't believe me?" she asked.

"I do," Brad said.

"How many were there?" I asked.

"Ten. Ten tarantulas. No, wait." She closed her eyes and tried to remember. "Eleven! There were eleven because the last one had a baby riding on her back."

"Were they big?" Brad asked.

"Big and hairy," she said. "One hairier than the next."

"Aw, Grandma," Nate said, "you're fibbing!"

"She's not fibbing!" Cyn said, snuggling close to Grandma.

"She's NOT!" Teddy yelled. Grandma shushed him.

"Think I'd make up something like that?" she asked.

"Yeah." Nate smiled. "When I was little you used to tell the story about those five bad guys who kidnapped you and you had a gun but only one bullet so you told them to line up and then you shot them all with one bullet. I *know* that's not true."

"Did I say that?" Grandma looked surprised. "Well, maybe that one stretched the truth a little. But every word of the tarantula story is true."

"Tell us a story about when you were little," Cyn said. "Did you ever get in trouble?"

"Sometimes," Grandma admitted. "I got in trouble with the iceman once."

"The iceman?" I asked.

"Back when I was little we didn't have refrigerators

like we do today. We had something called an ice-box. And every couple days the iceman would come around. He had a wooden cart pulled by a horse. A big block of ice was on that cart. We would buy ice from the iceman. He'd use his ice pick to chip off a chunk of ice and then he'd carry it up and put it in our icebox."

"Aw, c'mon, Grandma," Nate said.

"It's true," she said.

"Didn't it melt?" I asked.

"After a while. When it melted we'd have to buy another piece of ice. My friends and I loved to sneak up and spy on the iceman. While he loaded up his ice and carried it up to our apartment, we'd run over to his cart." She dropped her voice to a whisper. "We'd steal little chunks of ice! And one summer day, a wicked hot day in August, the iceman caught me! He caught me with a piece of ice in my hands!"

"Did you get in trouble?" Teddy asked, smiling.

"He dragged me by my ear up to our apartment and told my father what I'd done."

"Did you get spanked on your bottom?" Brad asked.

"'Deed I did. My father gave me a licking I'll never forget!"

"Did he use his hand?" Nate asked.

"No, he took off his belt," Grandma said.

"Then his pants fell down." Nate giggled.

"He smacked me three times on the bottom, and I never stole another thing in my life."

"Did you cry?" Cyn asked.

"You bet I did." Grandma looked at Nate. "Does that story sound true?"

"Well, yeah," Nate said. "That one sounds a lot truer than the one about the tarantulas."

"Did I ever tell you about the time a swarm of honeybees came down our chimney?" Grandma asked.

"Aw, c'mon, Grandma . . ."

When the dough had risen, Grandma made us all wash our hands before we got to pound down the warm dough. We rolled it out, added the nuts and raisins and cherries, rolled it up again, and tucked the loaves into loaf pans so the dough could rise one more time.

Finally, the stollen went into the oven. Within minutes this incredible smell spread through the house.

The bread had to be eaten right away—within twenty-four hours—or it would start getting stale. Those first slices of stollen were so good they took the words out of our mouths. All we could do was eat. Nobody spoke. I finished two thick slices and pushed my plate back at Grandma for seconds. Just then the kitchen door flew open, letting in a blast of freezing cold air.

"DAD!" Teddy yelled.

First Uncle Billy and Dad came into the kitchen,

pulling the bottom stump of a Christmas tree, then a mass of green branches appeared, and, last of all, Mom, red-faced and smiling, holding the top of the tree. Dad stood the tree in the middle of the kitchen so we could all take a good look at it.

"Ain't she a beauty?" Dad asked.

At that Teddy jumped up, wagged his finger at Dad, and started chanting loudly:

> "Ain't, ain't, don't say ain't!
> Your mother will faint
> And your father will fall
> In a bucket of paint!"

"Shhh," Mom told him.

With the door shut we got our first strong whiff of that piney smell. Grandma's eyes widened at the sight of the tree.

"What do you think, Mother?" Mom asked Grandma.

"Well, Lisa, I do not believe I have ever seen a more lovely tree in my entire life." Grandma spoke slowly; it sounded funny, hearing my mother's real name spoken out loud. She walked around the tree. Then her eyes narrowed. She looked at my father and asked in a low voice: "How much did it cost?"

"A lot," Dad admitted.

"How much?" Grandma persisted.

"Seven dollars," Dad said with a straight face. A lie! I'd bought Christmas trees with Dad before, and

I knew very well that a tree like this would cost at least twenty dollars, maybe more.

"Seven dollars!" Grandma exclaimed. "The robbers!" She shook her head and walked around to take another slow look at it. "I guess the price of everything is going up these days. And it *is* a lovely tree. But seven dollars? If that isn't highway robbery, I don't know what is!"

The stollen, like any good food in our house, didn't last very long. Grandma promised she'd make another batch, but the next day she made pinwheel cookies instead. She had a tray ready to go into the oven when I noticed Josh curled up under the kitchen table. Lying on his blanket, sound asleep. That seemed strange—he'd already taken his nap. I touched his forehead and, boy, did it feel hot! I called to Mom: "Feel that! He's got a fever!"

Mom took his temperature. What she saw on the thermometer drained the blood from her face.

"Holy Mother of Mercy!" Mom yelled to Grandma. "A hundred five! Mother, am I reading that right?"

"Call the doctor," Grandma said. "You don't fool around with a fever like that."

Grandma carried Josh upstairs to Mom's bed while Mom called Dr. Wentworth. The doctor came over to the house, did a quick examination of Josh, and stood there, shaking his head.

"Don't like it one bit," said Dr. Wentworth. He was

a tall, bony man with huge hands, and he had this odd way of squeezing his hands when he talked. First his left hand squeezed his right hand; then his right squeezed his left.

"Cliff, wait in the kitchen for your father," Mom said. So I sat with Uncle Billy in the kitchen playing double solitaire. I could tell he was letting me win; he was making too many dumb mistakes. We had just started a fourth game when Dad walked into the kitchen carrying two big bags of groceries.

"Josh's really sick!" I told him. "Dr. Wentworth's up with him right now!"

Dad practically dropped the groceries onto the table and raced upstairs with me right behind. I stood in the bedroom doorway, feeling Nate and Cyn and Teddy breathing behind me. Dr. Wentworth was bent over Josh, listening with a stethoscope while Mom stroked Josh's forehead with a wet facecloth.

"What is it?" Dad asked Dr. Wentworth.

"That's the thing, I just plain don't know, and I'd be a liar if I pretended I did." Dr. Wentworth sighed, straightened up, and stood there rubbing his hands. "Looks like some sort of respiratory infection. Fever's still climbing, and his heartbeat's a little irregular. Not much, but enough to worry me. I don't like that."

"Well, what do you think?" Dad asked.

Dr. Wentworth paused again and bit his lower lip, hard. "Don't want to alarm you folks, but I think we better take him in to Good Sam."

I knew what that meant: Good Samaritan Hospital.

"Good Sam!" Mom cried.

"Just to be on the safe side," Dr. Wentworth said.

Dad and Mom looked at each other, then down at Josh. Dr. Wentworth had delivered all the babies in our family, including Josh. His words carried a lot of weight.

"All right," Dad said. "Let's go."

"Can I come?" I asked. Soon as I spoke the other kids crowded around Dad, talking all at once.

"Yeah, can I?"

"Please, can I?"

"I wanna come!"

"No, you kids stay here with Uncle Billy," Dad said. "We'll be back soon."

"Cliff, you help your uncle," Mom said. She put her hand on my shoulder. "I'm counting on you."

In two minutes flat Dad, Mom, Grandma, and Dr. Wentworth had bundled Josh up and were carrying him out the front door.

For supper Uncle Billy fixed a pizza shaped like a Christmas tree. He got Teddy and Brad decorating it with green and black olive slices, red and green peppers, pickles, and pepperoni all smothered with grated cheese. It looked terrific when it came out of the oven but I couldn't finish even one slice. Uncle Billy let us all stay up until Mom and Dad came home that night. We stood at the big front window, watching for cars.

Finally, at eight thirty, Nate spotted our car. We watched Dad and Mom and Grandma get out and walk toward the house. No Josh. The door opened. They came inside, and for a moment they stood there looking at us looking at them. I got a funny feeling in my gut.

"Where is he?" I asked.

"He's going to be all right," Dad said. "His fever's come down a little. He's sleeping right now; that's what he needs."

"But where *is* he?"

"He's in the hospital," Mom said. "That's where he needs to be right now."

"But when can he come home?" Nate asked.

"Probably not for at least four or five days," Mom said. She took a deep breath. "Right now it doesn't look like he'll be home for Christmas."

"Not home for Christmas!" Cyn cried. "But that's not fair!"

"The important thing is that he's going to be all right," Mom said softly. She hugged Cyn against her. "I think we can go see him tomorrow morning."

No one spoke for a moment.

"Can we all come?" Cyn asked.

"Yes, sure," Dad said. For the first time he smiled a little. "We'll all go together."

Christmas Eve morning, at eight thirty, all of us except Grandma Annie and Uncle Billy jammed into the car. Good Samaritan Hospital was ten minutes away. I'd always thought of Good Sam as the happy place where mothers went to have their babies: every kid in our family had been born there. It felt strange going to visit someone who was really sick. We walked through the main door to the big desk with the word Visitors over it. A woman behind the desk shook her head firmly when she saw all of us.

"You can't all go up there," she said, still shaking her head. "There's a limit of two visitors at a time."

"I understand," Dad tried to explain. "But Dr. Wentworth said—"

"Two visitors at a time," the woman repeated. She pointed at Brad and Teddy. "And no small children. Hospital regulations. I don't make them."

Just when it looked like she and Dad were going to get into an argument, Dr. Wentworth walked into the waiting room. He spoke in a whisper to the woman. She sighed, shook her head some more, and looked away. Dr. Wentworth motioned for us to follow him. We got onto an elevator. Mom gave Dr. Wentworth a small smile, but he didn't smile back.

"I called in earlier this morning," he said. "Josh's fever is still running high. I want you all to understand that ahead of time. He's a very sick child."

Nobody said anything the rest of the way up. We followed Dr. Wentworth into pediatrics, a huge room with lots of cribs. I counted sixteen of them along the walls.

There was Josh. He was in the middle of his crib, still, lying on his stomach. His eyes were open. The skin on his face looked sweaty and red. He just lay still, too weak even to lift his head off the crib sheet.

"Mama," he said in a croaking sort of voice. "Daddy."

"Hello, honey," Mom whispered. "We've all come to see you."

"Mommy-Daddy," Josh croaked.

Mom reached in and scooped him up. Josh lay against her shoulder. She rocked him, closed her eyes, hummed to him, smiling with only her mouth. Dad whispered to Josh and rubbed his back. I moved around so I could see Josh's face. "Josh!" I whispered.

"Hi, Joshie!" Teddy said.

"Josh-u-a-Good-Boy!" Cyn said, touching his cheek.

Brad lifted himself up on tiptoes so he could give Josh a quick kiss. Josh stayed very still. Only his eyes moved, lighting on each one of our faces. He knew we were there, and I think he was glad of it, but he couldn't even manage a smile.

In a few minutes a nurse came over to the crib.

"I think we'd better let Josh try to sleep," she said.

"All right," Mom said. The nurse took Josh from her arms and put him back into the crib. Nobody spoke. The nurse put Josh onto his belly. He just lay there without moving.

"Mommy-Daddy," he said softly.

"Bye, Josh," Mom said, smiling and trying not to cry.

"Yes, he needs his sleep," Dr. Wentworth said.

We started to leave, but Mom stopped at the door.

"I want to stay," she said.

"There's really nothing you can do," Dr. Wentworth said.

"I know, I know," Mom said. "But it would just make me feel better to be with him. Maybe he'll sleep better knowing I'm nearby."

"It would be all right," the nurse said. "We could set up a little cot for you if you want to lie down."

"All right," Dad said. He gave Mom a kiss. "Call if there's any change."

The rest of us walked out, past the other rooms, past the nurses, went down the elevator, filed past the lady at the visitors' desk. Nobody spoke. Outside Good Sam, Dad talked to Dr. Wentworth for a minute. As soon as Brad got back into the car he started to cry.

"I want Josh," he said.

"He's going to be all right," Dad said. He touched the steering wheel and gripped it hard. "He's going to be all right. He's going to be all right."

The house stayed quiet. Grandma sat by the fireplace, knitting. Everybody else, except me, sat around watching TV. I went up to my room and sorted baseball cards, thumbing through a big stack, looking for all-stars. Later I went down past Dad and Mom's bedroom, and I could hear Dad talking in a low voice on the telephone.

A friend, Larry, called to invite me over to his house.

"Can't," I said. "My baby brother's real sick—he's at Good Sam." Boy, did it sound strange hearing such serious words—"he's at Good Sam"—come out of my mouth. It scared me.

"Oh, I'm sorry," Larry said, though he sounded more confused than sorry. A moment later we both hung up. I wished we could've talked longer, but I didn't know what to say.

Late in the afternoon Mom came back home. Josh was sleeping and could not be disturbed. We couldn't go back to the hospital until eight o'clock. That news sent a chill through the house. It was starting to get dark outside when Grandma called everyone into the kitchen.

"Under the circumstances," she said, "I thought we might need a family meeting. Now, we're all sad about Josh, but there's no sense moping around like it's the night before doomsday. He's right where he needs to be. And we need to get things ready around here."

"Grandma's right," Mom put in. "They're taking good care of Josh. But there's a lot that needs to get done right here."

"I'm not as young as I used to be—can't do it on my own," Grandma said. "I'm going to need some help." She looked at me hard. "We're going to make another batch of stollen. Cliff, can I count on you to help?"

For a moment I didn't answer. That word—stollen—hung in the air and it sounded exactly like *stolen*. Josh, twenty-two months old, stolen from us on Christmas Eve.

"I guess," I sighed. Making bread was about the last thing I felt like doing.

"Come on, then," Grandma retorted. "Let's get moving! Get the bag of flour—the unopened one—from the pantry."

With a great effort I pushed myself off my seat and shuffled into the pantry.

"C'mon!" Grandma called after me. "Last time I looked this was still Christmas Eve, and I don't have too many more left, let me tell you! At my age every one counts. C'mon, all of you put your stuff on this table. Shake a leg! Let's get organized. Cyn—eggs and the bag of sugar. Nate, get the yeast! Teddy? See if you can find me two sticks of butter in the fridge!"

Without a word, Teddy went to fetch the butter.

"Brad!"

"Cherries?" he said meekly, looking up.

"Cherries it is!" she said loudly. "And the raisins. And the walnuts. Can you carry all that?" Then, to Mom: "Lisa, where did I put that cup measure?"

Within minutes, the table was covered with the ingredients.

"That's more like it," Grandma said. "All right, everybody knows what to do? Go to it!"

"But, Grandma," Cyn said. "Who's going to mash the nuts?"

Cyn pointed to the bag of walnuts, unopened, sitting on the table. Grandma cleared her throat.

"Brad, why don't you chop the walnuts," Grandma

said. "When you're finished doing the cherries and raisins."

"No," Brad said. He looked down. "I can't."

"Why not?"

"I don't want to," Brad said.

"Well, how about you, Teddy?" Grandma asked. "Would you do it?"

"But . . ." Teddy hesitated. He shook his head.

There was a short pause.

"Well, maybe just for today your Uncle Billy can chop the nuts," Grandma said. "Bill, think you can manage that?"

"Uncle Billy *can't* mash the nuts," Cyn told Grandma quietly. "That's the baby's job. Only Josh can mash the nuts."

Cyn looked down. For a moment I thought she would cry. Everybody stayed quiet. I tried hard not to look at her. Or at the unopened bag of walnuts. Finally, Grandma spoke.

"Young lady, you're right, as usual," she said. "That's Josh's job, and nobody should do it for him. Here's my idea. How about this time we'll leave out the nuts. What do you say?"

Cyn looked up and nodded seriously.

"Anybody object to that?"

Pause.

"Good!" Grandma said. She put the walnuts back into the cabinet. She looked relieved. "That solves that problem."

The dough rose, got pounded down, got made

into loaves, and rose again. When Grandma put the loaves into the oven it wasn't fifteen minutes before that yeasty smell had taken over the house again.

After supper I hung my stocking over the fireplace. Uncle Billy put out a piece of pie for Santa Claus and some nice carrots for the reindeer. But instead of going to bed I piled into the cars along with every-one else and headed back to Good Sam. We took two cars this time because Grandma Annie and Uncle Billy came, too.

The lady at the visitors' desk nodded wearily at us and motioned to the elevator. Dr. Wentworth met us just outside pediatrics.

We hurried inside. Josh was sitting up! The skin on his face still looked hot and red, and his curls were sweaty, but his eyes looked much brighter.

"Mommy-Daddy!" he cried, in a clear voice.

"Well, hello!" Mom said. She lifted him out and turned to Dr. Wentworth. "He's better, isn't he?"

"Much better. Looks to me like he's turned the corner. The temperature's come down a lot. Boy, that was some kind of nasty infection he had. Never saw anything like it. He had me worried, but I think he's going to be all right. He's a skinny little feller, but he's a fighter."

Uncle Billy sidled up to Josh, tickled under his chin, and started play-boxing with him. "A fighter, are you? Well, then, put up your dukes. Put up your dukes!"

Josh grinned. He grinned at each of us. Mom passed him to Dad. Dad swung Josh around, like he was waltzing with him.

"Easy does it," Dr. Wentworth said. "He's still running a fever."

"Can't he come home with us?" Cyn asked Dr. Wentworth. "Please? That would be the best present of all."

"I'm sorry, no," Dr. Wentworth said. "He really needs to be here at least two more days, so we can watch him closely. But he's going to be all right, that's the main thing. He'll be home before you know it."

Mom and Dad took turns holding and hugging Josh. Then Grandma Annie hugged him.

"You had us all mighty worried, you skinny little chicken, you!" she told Josh.

"Hey, can I take him for a walk?" I asked after a minute. "He must hate being cooped up in that crib."

"I don't know," Mom said doubtfully, but Dr. Wentworth nodded at her. "Well, all right. But not too far. Stay inside this room."

When she handed Josh to me he felt light as a bird. The other kids crowded around, touching his fingers and feet, jabbering at him all at once. Teddy and Brad started singing: "We WISHHHHHH you a merry Christmas," in a soft, funny way, suddenly bringing their faces close to Josh's on the word *wish*. Josh squirmed with delight. We all joined in:

"We WISHHHHHH you a merry Christmas
We WISHHHHHH you a merry Christmas . . . "

The six of us walked toward the far end of the room where there was a door, half-open. Inside we could see two sets of bunk beds, each with a small wooden ladder leading up to the top bunk. All of a sudden Josh started gasping. He was pointing at the wooden ladder; I could feel his whole body trembling with excitement.

"A yidda yadda!" he cried. "A yidda yadda!"

Nate, Cyn, Teddy, Brad and I stood there staring stupidly at the ladder.

"A little ladder!" we all said in unison. "A little ladder!"

Josh beamed at me and at everyone else. Nate, Teddy, and Brad started laughing and raced back to where the grown-ups were still talking to Dr. Wentworth. They dragged them back to the little room so Josh could repeat it again.

"I wanna yidda yadda," he said, pointing at one of the wooden ladders.

"A little ladder," Cyn said with a big smile. "See? That's what he's been trying to tell us all along. He wants a little ladder for Christmas!"

"Well, for heaven's sake!" Mom said, shaking her head. She took Josh from me and passed him over to Grandma Annie.

"What on earth does a kid that age want a ladder for?" Uncle Billy wondered.

"We have to get him one," I whispered to Dad, pulling him aside. "We have to, Dad. Really."

"Not tonight we can't," Dad said. "The stores are all closed. It's Christmas Eve."

"Wait a second, Clifford," Uncle Billy said to Dad. "Give me a second here." He closed his eyes. Rubbed his chin. At that moment I half-expected him to say something silly, but he didn't. "You've got power tools, don't you?"

"Some," Dad said.

"Any lumber down in the basement?"

"Some two-by-fours, but you're not—"

"Oh I am, I am!" Uncle Billy said. He clapped his hands loudly together and the sound—POCK!—echoed through the hospital room. His eyes had a bright and devilish gleam. "We can *make* that little ladder. Build it ourselves."

"Tonight?" Dad said. "For heaven's sake, man, it's nine o'clock. You're crazy!"

"I've been called that and a lot worse than that," Uncle Billy replied with a smile that showed all his teeth. "You got sandpaper? Got any wood stain?"

"You are serious," Dad said, starting to grin himself. "Can you really build it?"

"*We* can build it," Uncle Billy corrected him. He walked over to inspect the little ladder. "Sure. Something like this should be easy. Piece of cake."

"I'm helping!" Teddy announced.

"Me, too," Nate said.

"Can I help, please?" I asked. "I'm taking shop in school—"

"I want to help, too!" Cyn said.

Dad looked at Uncle Billy, then at Mom. They were both smiling. Dad shook his head.

"You kids *should* go to bed, but I've got a funny feeling you wouldn't be able to fall asleep anyway," Dad said. "All right, we'll build a ladder for Josh. Even if it takes us all night!"

We let out a cheer.

"Shhh!" Mom said. "This is a hospital!"

"All right, everyone, say good-bye to Josh," Dad said. Then, to Mom: "We're going to need us a couple pots of strong coffee."


We went home and crowded into the basement. There, under Uncle Billy's expert direction, we spent the next three hours making a ladder. Nate and I took turns cutting with the power saw, but everyone helped. We spent the time measuring, planning, cutting, drinking coffee or hot chocolate, fitting, adjusting, eating stollen and apple pie, recutting, singing, sweeping, laughing, sanding, telling stories, wiping, imagining Josh's reaction, staining, admiring. It got later and later, ten, eleven, way past midnight, but nobody seemed to get tired, not even Grandma. I felt as if I could've stayed up all night.

"That's one heckuva of a ladder," Uncle Billy said when we were done.

And it was: a gleaming piece of furniture, about three and a half feet high, with four evenly spaced rungs. Teddy tried it out and pronounced it fit to climb. We brought it upstairs so Grandma could put a bright blue-and-white ribbon bow on each rung.

"I'm not sure why he needs a little ladder," Mom said, "and I'm half afraid he's going to fall off and break his neck. But if that's what he wants, that's what he's going to get!"

Christmas morning, eight o'clock sharp. I was eager to open my presents, but more eager to see Josh's reaction. I jumped into my clothes, and we headed back to Good Sam.

We all carried the ladder into the pediatric ward: Cyn in front, me and Brad on one side, Nate and Teddy on the other. Josh was awake. When he saw us, when he saw the ladder, he pulled himself into a standing position and pointed, eyes wide, mouth open in astonishment, grinning so hard I thought his cheeks might crack right off.

"A yidda yadda!" he cried. "A yidda yadda!"

# 3. Under the Kitchen Table

Grandma Annie liked to say that Teddy was born with "the heebie-jeebies in his veins and his brains." I couldn't agree more, and I should know because I've baby-sat him, plenty. Lots of times Dad and Mom went out shopping, they'd take the baby and put me "in charge" of the other kids. That wouldn't have been half bad if it hadn't been for Teddy. He could make any baby-sitter miserable because he never slowed down and he never stopped coming up with new ways of getting into trouble.

One time Mom asked me to baby-sit the other kids while she took Brad to the doctor's. All Teddy did was "feed" the fish by dumping Cheerios into their bowl. He took Cyn's jewelry and put it onto her stuffed animals. He tossed Mom and Dad's toothbrushes into the toilet. When Mom got back, Teddy got into trouble and I got into trouble, too, for not minding him better.

"You've got to keep a closer eye on Teddy," Mom told me.

What was I supposed to do: put him in a strait-jacket? Tie him up? There are laws against stuff like that.

Take how Teddy acted on New Year's Day when we were at Aunt Pat and Uncle Arthur's house for their big holiday feast.

The holiday feast was a combination dinner where each family brought one major dish, or dessert. Just thinking about it made my mouth water. Uncle Eddie always fixed spaghetti with a thick sausage and meatball sauce. Aunt Pat and Uncle Arthur had spent a dozen years in South Carolina. Uncle Arthur always made his famous she-crab bisque; Aunt Pat fixed fried chicken with sweet potato biscuits. Aunt Marilyn always baked these delicious little dough pockets, some stuffed with meat, others with spinach and onions and mint. Grandma Annie usually made a couple blueberry pies, plus a double batch of stollen.

We always made fig pudding. Or, I should say, Dad made it. He had a friend from college, a guy who grew prize-winning figs on his farm in California. Just before the holidays, a UPS truck pulled up in front of our house with a box of figs as it did every year. On Saturday, the day before the feast, Dad cooked.

As a cook, Dad was the exact opposite of Grandma. Grandma invited everyone into the kitchen. She handed out jobs; she put you to work. Dad called himself a "solo artist" and he insisted on cooking alone.

"Out! Out!" he yelled, shooing us from the kitchen. "A great chef needs to focus! A great chef needs to concentrate!"

"Yeah, Dad, we know what a great chef needs," I teased him, "but don't you think *you* could use a little help?"

"A great chef," Dad sniffed, "is often not appreciated by his family!"

He spent all afternoon in there surrounded by bowls, mixer, figs, eggs, molasses, lemon, buttermilk, walnuts, cinnamon, nutmeg, brown sugar, and confectioners' sugar. It looked like a mess, but Dad knew what he was doing: he could make one mean fig pudding. While he chopped, stirred, and mixed we could hear him singing:

> "Now bring out the figgy pudding
> Now bring out the figgy pudding
> Now bring out the figgy pudding
> Now bring it right here!
>
> We won't go until we get some
> We won't go until we get some
> We won't go until we get some
> So bring it right here!"

The whole family was in a great good mood: Josh

had just gotten out of the hospital a couple days before.

"At Aunt Pat and Uncle Arthur's house we can celebrate having Josh back with us," Mom said.

But it didn't work out that way, mostly because of Teddy. The moment we arrived Teddy started running through the house and he didn't stop running until it was time to eat. Then he clowned around at the table by licking his plate. Mom made him stop, but when it was time for dessert Teddy threw a glob of fig pudding that landed on the white dress of Rebecca, our eight-year-old cousin.

After dinner Teddy raced through the living room and knocked two glasses of punch off the coffee table. Mom put Teddy on "Time Out."

"Too much sugar," Aunt Ruth suggested.

"Too much Christmas," Mom put in.

"Just the heebie-jeebies," Grandma said. "He'll outgrow it."

Later, when Teddy bit cousin Sheila on the arm, I knew it was time to leave. We got into the car and started home. Five minutes later Teddy was fast asleep.

"Finally!" Dad whispered.

"Mom, why was Teddy so awful today?" Cyn whispered. "If they had a jail for second graders, he'd be in it. He's like the baddest kid in the world."

"Not bad, just wild," Mom replied. "I guess some people are born that way."

Amen. Teddy was born wild. The way Mom tells it, Teddy never really learned to walk. At eleven months he pulled himself up into a standing position and started running around the house. He fell a lot but he could still move fast. And once Teddy could move, nobody was safe.

Teddy was wild in church, wild in school, and especially wild during the holidays. After Christmas, while Josh was still at Good Sam, Teddy started hiding people's presents and unscrewing lights on the tree. He took globs of silvery tinsel off and made little bird nests that he stuck back onto the tree. One day while Mom and Dad were shopping Teddy stole the baby Jesus from the manger and laughed when no one could find it. See what I'm saying? He stole Jesus and thought it was funny.

Grandma Annie always said that Teddy had "the eyes of a priest." Ha! "The eyes of a devil" is a lot more like it.

After Josh came home from the hospital, Mom and Dad figured Teddy would calm down. Wrong. If anything, Teddy got worse. Some of his pranks made me laugh, like the time he stuck a cold fried chicken leg under Cyn's pillow. But when he started messing with my stuff I stopped laughing.

He stole my collection of all-star baseball cards and took them outside in dead winter. I found them blowing across the backyard like a bunch of dry leaves.

Teddy got punished for that, but the following week he was at it again. This time he took my prized marble: a huge crystal mumbo, pale silver, with a piece of netting at the center. He stole the marble off my bureau, brought it to school, and actually traded it to a sixth grader named Spencer Harris for a stopwatch. When I found out about that I decided to unscrew his greasy little head once and for all, and I would've done it except that Dad stepped in. He called up Spencer Harris and made him trade back. Then Dad gave Teddy a long lecture about "respecting other people's belongings."

I knew that wouldn't help, and it didn't. In the middle of February Teddy took my new Lionel train engine outside and left it on the back porch. I found it frozen solid to the snow.

"Mom!" I screamed. "I'm gonna murder that kid!"

Mom did what she always did: she sent Teddy straight up to his bedroom. But this time Teddy sort of went berserk. He opened his bedroom window and started throwing stuff—books, clothes, coat hangers—down onto the yard below.

"That's it!" Mom yelled. "I've had it! The worm has turned!"

She dragged Teddy downstairs, into the kitchen, and made him sit under the kitchen table. "You stay under there!" she said. "Here at least I can keep an eye on you!"

"How long?" he whimpered.

"Till I say!" she shot back.

"How long is that?"

"I don't know how long," Mom told him. "I haven't decided. Right now I just want you to think about how you've been behaving around here."

Teddy put on his poutiest face, but I didn't feel sorry for him. The way I figured it, he deserved this punishment—and a lot more.

"But how *long*?" Teddy asked again.

"A year," I muttered. "Maybe two."

"SHUT UP!" Teddy screamed at me.

And that's how it started. Whenever Teddy got into serious trouble, which he did at least once a day, Mom put him under the kitchen table.

"Can I go now?" he'd ask after a little while. "I'll be good."

"That's what you always say," Mom said, shaking her head. But after a while she always let him go.

When the school bus came come one morning Teddy hid behind a tree and it left without him.

Under the kitchen table.

Teddy found Brad's toy car lying beside the driveway. It was a little red plastic Jeep with a hood that could open and shut, and a little man seated behind the steering wheel. When no one was looking Teddy wedged the toy Jeep behind the back wheel of Mom's car. Later, when she backed her car down the driveway, Brad's Jeep—and driver—got flattened together like a pancake. Brad started wailing nonstop.

And Teddy went under the kitchen table.

The strange thing was that Teddy never tried to hide the truth about what he'd done.

"Did you put Brad's truck under there?" Mom asked.

"Yeah," he admitted.

"Did you know the car would break?"

"I guess."

"You guess?"

"Yeah," he said. "I knew."

"How would you like someone to break one of *your* favorite toys?"

Silence. Then: "I wouldn't."

"Why did you do that?"

"I don't know."

Some days I did feel a little sorry for Teddy, with his round head and pudgy belly and crew-cut hair, resting his chin in his hands, crying a little but mostly just looking sad or mad or glum. He spent lots of time under the kitchen table—at times it seemed like he practically *lived* under there.

One day a friend telephoned for Teddy while he was under the kitchen table.

"Can't play right now," Teddy whispered into the phone. "I'm back in the *dungeon*."

Teddy was under the kitchen table when the plumber came to fix the kitchen pipes. He was sitting under there when old Mrs. Reamsnyder and old Mr. Hollis came over after church on Sunday morning. He was sitting under there when my best friend,

Larry Greene, came over to play. Nobody thought much about it.

One morning Mom couldn't find a couple squares of yeast she needed to bake bread. She searched the kitchen twice.

"I know I bought that yeast," she said, chewing her bottom lip. "It's got to be around here someplace."

Teddy ran into the room and Mom grabbed him by the arm before he could scoot by.

"Teddy, have you seen a couple little packets of yeast?"

By way of answer Teddy walked over to the refrigerator, reached behind it, and pulled out two shiny packets. Mom lowered her head and gave him a suspicious look.

"Did you put it there? Please tell me the truth."

"No, Mom! See, yesterday when I was, you know, sitting under the table, I thought I saw something shiny back there but I didn't know what it was."

"Well, good thing you kept your eyes peeled," Mom said to him. "Looks like we'll be having bread tonight after all!"

A few weeks later Mom was trying to decide what to buy Mrs. Reamsnyder for a birthday present.

"What on earth does a seventy-four-year-old woman want or need?" Mom asked.

"Socks," Teddy said. "That woman needs socks, real bad. Her socks have more holes than Swiss cheese!"

"When did you notice that?" she asked.

"When I was . . ." Teddy pointed: under the kitchen table.

So Mom bought Mrs. Reamsnyder three bright new pairs of cotton socks.

"Perfect, perfect, perfect!" Mrs. Reamsnyder said when she opened the present. "Socks are exactly what I needed. How on earth did you know?"

A couple weeks later we were sitting around the kitchen table eating blueberry pancakes for breakfast.

"Know what?" Teddy asked. "I think Mr. Hollis and Mrs. Reamsnyder are going to get married."

"Yeah, sure." I laughed. True, he was a widower and she a widow, but they were both ancient.

"I don't think so," Mom said, smiling. "They're both a little too old to get married. Mr. Hollis must be close to eighty by now. Sometimes a man and a woman stay good friends without ever getting married."

Three weeks later it came in the mail: a *wedding invitation*! Old Mrs. Reamsnyder and Mr. Hollis were actually going to tie the knot. The rest of us were in total shock.

"How on earth did you know?" Dad asked Teddy.

"From sitting under the kitchen table," he said. "Last time they came over I was sitting under there and I saw them holding hands. Secret-like."


It would be great if the story could end there with

everybody amazed at all the things Teddy noticed and him just sort of outgrowing having to sit under the kitchen table. The way a snake outgrows its skin.

But it didn't happen that way. True, Teddy got famous in our house for the stuff he'd notice. But Teddy's sharp eyes didn't keep him out of trouble. One morning at school, in late February, he dared this little kid, Paul Anniboli, to lick the ice-cold metal bar on the jungle gym. Of course the kid's tongue got stuck there, frozen solid to the metal.

"Don't move!" Teddy told him, but the kid panicked and pulled away and left a bunch of tongue skin stuck to the metal pole. When Teddy got home he got sent back under the kitchen table.

In mid-March we got a sudden snap of warm weather. Brad took a blanket out to the backyard and lay down to read his favorite book about his favorite subject: horses. The book was a present from Grandma Annie, *Horses Around the World*, with lots of beautiful photographs. When Teddy saw Brad reading, he ran up to him.

"Mom needs to talk to you," Teddy said.

That was a lie, of course, but it would never occur to gullible Brad that anyone would lie to him. He ran inside and left the horse book lying on the grass. Teddy found a big fat green caterpillar. He opened the book, dropped in the caterpillar and—SPLAT!— slammed the pages shut. When Mom heard about it she dragged Teddy into the kitchen.

"Back there?" Teddy asked. He pointed under the kitchen table.

"Nope," Mom said. She shook her head. "No more."

He looked up, surprised. "Why not?"

"Doesn't work," Mom said. "All the time you've spent sitting under that table hasn't helped make you act any better. What's the use? We'll have to think of something else."

"I'm a free man!" Teddy cried. "A free man!"

"Yes," Mom said. "But you ruined Brad's book, Mr. Free Man. I'm going to find out how much it cost. And you are going to pay back every cent of it. Do you understand me?"

"Yeah."

A few days later Teddy was back under the kitchen table, surrounded by about twenty stuffed animals.

"What are you doing under there?" Mom asked. "You didn't do anything wrong. You're a free man, remember?"

"Havin' a circus," he said. "The table is my circus tent."

The next day Teddy and Brad took their plastic soldiers under the kitchen table and had a war. The day after that Teddy and Brad set up a food store under the kitchen table. They played for hours. All this made no sense to me. I finally said to Teddy: "Didn't you hear what Mom said? You don't *have* to stay under there. You can play wherever you want."

"So?" Teddy just shrugged.

"So why hang around here?" I asked. "You've got the whole house to play in."

"It's cool under here," Teddy said. "I'm used to it. It's like my favorite place in the whole house."

When I mentioned this conversation to Mom, she just looked at me, slowly shaking her head.

"That's what I was afraid of," she said.

# 4. The Tackle Box

On April fifth I turned twelve and got the best present ever: a fishing tackle box. I fell in love with it—the solid weight, the six little drawers made of clear hard plastic so you could see the stuff inside. There were extra hooks in one drawer, sinkers in another, extra fishing line in a third, bobbers in a fourth, fishing lures in the fifth. In the sixth drawer I found a brand-new fishing knife with a jagged blade snug in its own leather pouch.

For my birthday Dad took me and Nate and three of my friends to Fenway Park in Boston. We watched the Sox pound the Yankees eleven to five (I almost caught a foul ball) and came home for pizza and cake and ice cream and presents. After I had opened the tackle box I started looking forward to everyone going home.

After the last kid left I took the tackle box up to my

bedroom, closed the door, and put it on my bed. I'd never seen anything so beautiful. I opened it up and took out the gear. I spread everything out in separate piles, taking care not to get the piles mixed up.

I figured the best place to keep my tackle box would be under my bed. It had to be a safe place where people (Teddy) couldn't get into it. Nate and I shared the bedroom but I never worried about him. He didn't mess around with my stuff, and I didn't mess around with his, especially his junk.

Nate collected junk. He was famous for it. If you peeked into his junk drawer you'd see all sorts of weird things: big metal bolts, a drop line with sinker, trilobite fossils, a bird's skull, a rusty hubcap, a broken gyroscope, links from a bike chain, a chunk of fool's gold, a golf ball with the cover ripped off, quartz crystals, arrowheads, wires, watch gears, ball bearings.

Just then Nate came into the bedroom.

"That's cool," he said, touching the tackle box's smooth red side. "That would be perfect to store my junk."

I shot him a look.

"Just kidding. Hey, can I come fishing when you go?"

"Yeah, I guess."

"When?"

"When Dad takes me," I said. "Whenever that is."

Nate's question got me thinking. Later that night I asked Dad, "When can we go fishing?"

"Maybe next week," he said. "Right now I'm just buried alive at work."

But next week when I asked Dad again he gave me the same answer: "Later."

One Saturday morning I took my rod, reel, and tackle box outside. There was no water around our house, no streams, no creeks or ponds, but there were plenty of woods behind the house. A warm spring day. I walked along and after a while I came to a grassy clearing where the trees ended and the sun poured in.

I sat down, opened the box, took out a sinker, and tied it onto the end of the line. I cast the line out onto the grass. It sailed through the sunlight and landed on the far side of the clearing. I cranked the handle of my reel—the sinker skittered along the grass when I reeled back. I did it again, and again: cast out, reel back in, cast out, reel back in. It was fun. There was a rhythm to it, like playing tennis or pitching in a baseball game.

At first I felt a little silly, fishing in the grass, but after a while I completely forgot where I was. The grass became the ocean. The crows flying overhead turned into seagulls. The tall pine trees at the edge of the clearing swayed in the wind like masts on a ship.

One time I cast too far; the line and sinker got snagged in the branches of a tree, and I had to take out the fishing knife to cut the line down.

"Hey, how's it going? Fish biting?"

I turned around: Nate.

"You following me?" I asked. "Beat it!"

"Nope, just out walking." He grinned. "Catch anything so far? You bring your fishing license?"

"Very funny."


One day in late May, Nate and I were playing catch in the backyard while Dad worked in the garage, putting up shelves. Dad is real tall—"just one long drink of water," Grandma likes to say—and the shelves would be up high where us kids couldn't reach them. It was strange seeing Dad working with a drill because he wasn't that good at building things. Not like my friend Joe McDonough's father, who built a new garage on their house all by himself. Dad was the first to admit that he wasn't great with tools. "My favorite tool is the telephone," he joked, meaning he'd use it to call the carpenter or plumber when something around the house needed fixing. Dad was good at other things, though—he was an expert on the history of the Civil War. He'd written lots of articles about it. I once saw him give a speech to a crowd of people, a hundred or even more, all of them listening and writing down stuff he said. No way Mr. McDonough could do something like that.

Now Dad put down his drill and called us over. "You guys get your gear ready," he said.

"Gear?"

"*Fishing* gear," Dad said. "Tomorrow morning we're

going out on a fishing boat to catch us a mess of fish!"

"All right!" Nate said, slapping my hand so hard it hurt, and the hurt felt good. We raced into the house.

The next day Dad and Nate and I got up early, packed the car, and left the house with empty stomachs. We drove about five miles and stopped at a restaurant just as the sun was coming up, all of us hungry as grizzlies. Nate loved meat, and he wanted to order the "Astronaut Breakfast"—steak and eggs. Dad said no to that but he did let us order the "Lumberjack Special": eggs, bacon, pancakes, juice, hot chocolate for us, coffee for him.

At the fishing dock there were about a dozen fishing boats lined up.

"That's our boat," Dad said, pointing at one of the boats. "*Captain Bob*."

The *Captain Bob* looked brand-new: clean white sides, crisp red lettering in back, and a flying bridge. We went on board. There were about ten of us including the captain, a big guy with a red veiny face and watery eyes. The guy looked older than Dad, but maybe it was just that his face was weathered from being out on the ocean. He was wearing a Pittsburgh Steelers cap.

"You must be Captain Bob," Dad said, reaching out to shake the man's hand.

"I won't argue with that," Captain Bob said, smiling back. He crunched the bones in my hand when he shook it. "What's the occasion? Birthday?"

"Well, sort of," I said.

"Sort of a delayed birthday present," Dad put in. "We're hoping to catch some real fish."

"I think I can arrange that," Captain Bob said. "Welcome aboard!"

Captain Bob unhooked the lines and backed the boat out of the dock slip. We traveled slowly out into the ocean. A perfect day: no clouds and barely any wind. The ocean looked like a huge sheet of glass someone had spent the night polishing. I stood in the back at the rail, watching the little cloud of seagulls chasing our boat.

In about a half hour Captain Bob cut the engine, threw in the anchor, and—BANG! We hardly had our lines in the water a half minute before the man next to me had hooked a fish. Then another guy's rod got tugged down.

"Got one!" Nate cried. "Whoa!"

I felt a heavy tug on my line.

"Me, too!" I cried.

"Bluefish!" Captain Bob yelled. "They run in schools! Keep your tips up!"

I tried to crank my reel but it was hard. I could feel my fish under the water thrashing wildly.

"Reel it in nice and steady!" Dad yelled. He was struggling with his rod, too.

Finally, after about five minutes, I got my fish reeled in far enough so I could see the silver, shadowy shape just beneath the surface.

"Easy," Captain Bob said. He reached down and used a long hook to pull it in. The bluefish was thick and as long as my arm.

"Nice fish, son!" Captain Bob said, slapping me on the back. "Gave you some fight, didn't she? Oh, do I love blues! They ain't much for eating, but for my money pound for pound they're the best fighting fish in the sea!"

Nate landed his fish and then hooked a bigger bluefish that gave him such a fight Dad had to step in and finish pulling it up. I hooked something called a weakfish even though it didn't feel weak—it nearly pulled my arms off. Everybody on the boat was catching fish, straining with their bent rods, with Captain Bob skipping from one side of the boat to the other pulling in fish with his long hook.

On the way home the inside of our car had a nice fishy smell. My jeans were streaked with dried fish blood. I felt happy and a little bit sunburned and bone tired. I'd caught thirteen fish, Nate eleven, and Dad four, not counting all the fish he'd helped us with.

"Have a good time?" Dad asked.

"Yeah, great!"

"I haven't been fishing for ages," Dad said.

"Good thing we had the tackle box," Nate put in.

True: we'd had to replace a bunch of lost hooks and sinkers. Twice Dad had used the fishing knife to cut off some tangled line.

"You said it," Dad said. He turned to the backseat to look at me. "Cliff, I want to borrow your tackle box so I can take the other kids out fishing tomorrow."

Those words—*borrow your tackle box*—gave me a weird feeling in my belly. I stared forward. I opened my mouth to say something, but my throat had frozen up. I couldn't speak. The feeling in my stomach kept getting stronger, and after a few minutes I realized that it was an awful lot like a stomachache.

Nate's friend, Ricky Topham, was waiting in the kitchen. Nate gave Mom his bag of fish and raced off with Ricky.

"I just wonder what we're going to have for dinner," Mom said to me. "Ugh, you smell awful! Have a good time?"

"Yeah, great," I said. Truth was, I didn't feel so great.

I didn't eat much supper. Captain Bob was right: bluefish looked a lot better than they tasted. Afterward I carried the tackle box up the two flights of stairs to my bedroom. The room was empty: Nate was downstairs watching TV.

I put the tackle box on my bed and opened it. Some of the hooks and sinkers had gotten mixed together during the trip, and I spent a few minutes putting the gear back in the right place. The fishing knife had some dried fish guts on the blade and dried fish scales on its protective case, and I carefully cleaned that stuff off.

When the tackle box was back in order and everything was exactly the way it had been before the fishing trip, I closed it, put it on my desk, and lay on my bed. I closed my eyes to think about the fishing trip. I tried to remember all the fun we'd had, but for some reason all I could see was Cyn and Teddy and Brad pawing through my tackle box, messing up the drawers, spilling sinkers, losing hooks, tangling up the fishing line. Fooling around with my fishing knife. I blinked a couple times, but hard as I tried, I couldn't get those pictures out of my head. I didn't mind the kids using my rod and reel, but the thought of them junking up my tackle box gave me a throbbing pain in my stomach.

I didn't know what to do.

An idea came into my head. I stood up, opened the tackle box, and started taking stuff out. I took out the extra hooks, the sinkers, the lures and bobbers and fishing line. The fishing knife. My heart was pounding something fierce. I hid all the fishing gear in the bottom drawer of my bureau, under the sweaters.

When the tackle box was empty, I went into the bathroom. At the back of the closet I found a bag of old cloth. I opened the bag and started stuffing cloth into the empty tackle box. Three diapers Josh had outgrown. Rags. Pieces from a white sheet that had been made into a ghost costume for Brad. Two pairs of old underwear full of holes. Six athletic socks. I jammed all of it into the tackle box and I kept stuffing in more and more until nothing else could fit. I closed the top. The tackle box felt heavy, like usual, when I picked it up. I put it in its usual spot under my bed.

I had trouble sleeping that night.

Next morning everyone got up early. While Mom made a picnic lunch, Dad fixed pancakes. But the little kids were so excited about going fishing they were practically bouncing off the walls. Josh and Brad rolled around under the kitchen table, wrestling and giggling. Cyn jumped up and down at the kitchen table, too excited to sit down or eat. Teddy grabbed Josh by his ears and started shouting: "DUMBO THE FLYING ELEPHANT! INTRODUCING DUMBO, THE FLYING ELEPHANT!"

Josh did have big ears. He was too little to understand about Dumbo, but he did know when he was being teased. Josh started to cry and tried to twist out of Teddy's grip. But Teddy wouldn't let go.

"Stop it!" I told Teddy and pulled them apart.

"All right, forget breakfast," Dad said. "Let's just pack up the car and go."

Mom brought out the lunch basket. Nate ducked into the garage to get the fishing rods: his, Dad's, mine. Teddy grabbed one of the rods and started cranking the reel.

"Don't!" Dad told him. "You're going to get the lines tangled before we get there!"

"Get into the car!" Mom told Teddy.

"Go up and get your tackle box," Dad told me.

I ran upstairs. My bedroom was perfectly quiet. When I picked up the tackle box and carried it downstairs, I felt strange, as if I was someone else.

"I'm gonna catch an electric eel!" Teddy was saying when I brought the tackle box to the car.

"I'm gonna catch a octopus," Brad said, "and Brandy's gonna catch a alligator." Brandy was Brad's doll, a little weird-looking bug-eyed elf with pointy ears and a bald head.

"Alligators don't live in the ocean," Cyn told him. "And you shouldn't bring Brandy fishing. He's gonna get fish guts on him!"

"I'm going and he's coming with me," Brad said.

I handed the tackle box to Dad. He put it next to him on the front seat of the car. The little kids piled into the backseat, Cyn and Teddy at the windows, Brad in the middle.

"Bye! Bye!" they yelled, waving madly at Mom, Nate, Josh, and me. Only Josh, who was in Mom's arms, didn't wave.

"I go," he said sadly.

"Next year," Mom told him. "When you're just a wee bit bigger."

The car moved slowly down the crushed-gravel driveway. Suddenly it stopped. Dad's window opened. He stuck out his head.

"Cliff!" he called. "Come over here."

I was already dead, my heart not beating, lungs not working, legs frozen to the ground. Somehow I made it over to the car. Dad gave me a short, hard look.

"Hold out your hand," he said.

I reached out, palm up, fingers spread. Dad put a five-dollar bill into my hand.

"Thanks," he said. He smiled. "Thanks for being generous enough to lend us your tackle box. Without that tackle box, there's no way I could be taking these kids fishing."

My throat was frozen. One last time I tried to say something, but Dad winked and drove away, the five-dollar bill fluttering like a wounded green butterfly in my hand.

"No sense us just hanging around here," Mom called. "It's going to be a hot one. Let's go to the beach. What do you say?"

"Yes!" Nate shouted.

"Beach!" Josh said.

"Cliff, how about you?"

"I guess," I said.


Nate and I were crazy about Brant Rock Beach: big waves, a fishing jetty you could walk way out on, plus a concession stand with plenty of ice cream and cold soda. At low tide you could explore thousands of little tidepools.

"Tide's out!" Nate yelled as soon as we hit the

beach. "Wanna check for sea worms?" Fishermen would pay a dollar a dozen for live sea worms, but you had to be careful: the worms could deliver a nasty bite.

"Worms!" Josh exclaimed.

"Nah," I said, spreading out my towel.

"Why not?" Nate asked.

"Just don't," I said. I lay down on my towel and let the hot sun beat down on my back.

"Wanna swim, then?" Nate asked.

"Swim!" Josh said.

"Nope," I said.

"Anybody want a nice cold juicy peach?" Mom said. "Cliff?"

"Nope," I said. "Not hungry. I don't think I'll be hungry all day."

"You're not sick, are you?" she asked. I started to tell her no but when I opened my mouth words started pouring out, fast and low and mumbly, before I could stop them. "Dad's gonna have trouble with the tackle box. Last night I took everything out."

"What?" Mom asked, leaning forward. "I don't think I heard you right."

"I said that last night I took all the fishing stuff out of the tackle box." I spoke louder this time. I didn't look at her but I could feel Mom staring at me.

"You gave him the tackle box *empty*?"

"I filled it with old diapers and other stuff."

"Really?" Nate said. He had a surprised, almost happy look on his face.

65

"You have anything to do with this?" Mom asked him.

"Me?" Nate threw up his arms. "No way! I—"

"I did it myself," I said.

"Why?" Mom demanded. "That doesn't sound like you. Why would you do something like that?"

"I was mad," I said, talking down at my towel. That sounded pretty lame, but I didn't know what else to say.

"Waves!" Josh cried, pointing at the ocean.

For a moment Mom was quiet. She stood up, took Josh's hand, and began walking with him down to the water. She took a few steps and turned around to look at me.

"Well, Clifford, I expect your father will want to talk to you when he gets home."

I know that, I thought, lying facedown on my towel. Tell me something I *don't* know.

We didn't stay at the beach very long, and that suited me fine. Back home, I changed from my bathing suit back into shorts and a baseball T-shirt.

I went up to my room. Only two o'clock. Dad probably wouldn't be home until five. Three long hours, and I knew they'd be tough hours to kill. I walked over and stood in front of the mirror above my dresser. My face stared back at me: Mr. Responsibility. Mr. Set-a-Good-Example. I felt awful.

Most days I avoided mirrors at all cost. I had Mom's brown eyes and Dad's big ears, not as big as Josh's, maybe, but big enough that I'd been teased a few times. It was weird seeing Mom's eyes and Dad's elephant ears stuck onto my own face. I had a ton of freckles, a little pug nose—hardly a nose at all—and, worst, this spiraling cowlick in my hair dead center above my forehead. It looked okay on my baby pictures, but now that I was older I hated it.

Nate came into the bedroom. He was a year younger than me and five pounds heavier. I would've traded my face for his in a second. It was as if he'd cherry-picked the best features from Mom and Dad. From Dad he got the bright blue eyes minus the big ears. He had Mom's straight blond hair. No pug nose. No freckles. And no cowlick.

"You're in big trouble," he said, lying on his bed with a little smirky smile on his face. It killed me seeing how much he was enjoying the situation.

"Thanks, Einstein," I replied coolly.

"What do you think Dad'll do?" he asked. "He might take your tackle box away forever."

I hadn't considered that, but I just shrugged as if I couldn't have cared less. I looked away, but my eyes snagged on something on top of my dresser.

The five-dollar bill.

It hurt to look at it. The bill was all curled and wrinkled. I picked it up and tried to smooth it out. Then I started to leave the room.

"Where you going?" Nate asked.

"None of your business," I said.

Mom and Dad's bedroom was empty. Downstairs in the kitchen I could hear Mom playing with Josh. I left the five-dollar bill on top of Dad's bureau.

"So what're you gonna do?" Nate asked when I returned.

"Don't you have someplace to go or something?" I asked him.

"Not really," Nate replied. He gave me one of those fake Cheshire cat grins.

"You're really starting to bug me."

"It's my room, too," Nate said.

"Thanks for reminding me."

Nate pulled out a comic book, but a few minutes later he put it away and left the room. I tried playing with my baseball cards. I'd been collecting since first grade, and I had a pretty big card collection, a shoebox and a half. But today it wasn't much fun looking through them. All the little numbers on the back started getting on my nerves, and it hit me that for a long time I hadn't really been having much fun with my baseball cards. I rubber-banded the stacks back together and carried them down to the den. Nate was watching TV.

"You want these?" I asked. I held out five neat stacks of cards.

He looked at me suspiciously. "All of them? How much?"

"For nothing. For free."

Nate's eyes grew wide.

"You don't want your cards anymore?"

"Nah," I said. "Kid stuff."

"Sure, I'll take them!" he said. "Hey, thanks!"

Upstairs again. I tried to read. I pretended to read. I wanted to read. I squinted at the page as though each word was a code to be cracked, but all the while I was listening for the sound of my father's car on the crushed-gravel driveway.

It started getting dark. Finally, after about a million years, I heard the sound of tires moving slowly on the driveway followed by the sound of a car engine. The engine turned off. Doors opened, slammed shut. The front door opened.

"Mom! Mom!" Teddy's voice. "We got fish!"

A whole minute passed. Then, a deeper voice from the bottom of the stairs: "Clifford? Come on down here!"

Dad.

I pulled myself off my bed and started coming down. Two flights of stairs. I made myself go at a regular speed, and I counted the stairs on the way down. Twenty-two steps. I wished it had been two thousand and twenty-two. Two million and twenty-two. I wished I could've gone down and down and down the stairs forever and never had to reach the bottom.

Dad was waiting in the kitchen. Standing. When Dad got mad he got quiet and serious. Now he stood in front of me looking very serious. It wasn't easy looking at him, so I tried looking at the fishing rods leaning against the table. I noticed that there was a key, like a car key or house key, jerry-rigged to one fishing line instead of a sinker, about eight inches from the hook. A bad sign.

The tackle box sat on the table. Just then I wished it hadn't been quite so bright and shiny. So red.

"Just one question," Dad said. "Why? Why did you do it?"

At that moment Brad came running into the kitchen.

"Hey, Cliff, we caught a lotta fish!" he yelled to me. Mom came in to get him.

"Come on," she said, leading him out. "Dad wants to talk to Cliff alone."

"Why?" Dad asked me. He wasn't yelling; Dad never yelled. Why had I done it? I'd only asked myself that question a thousand times that day.

"I'm sorry," I said. I shrugged and looked away.

"Mighty hard to keep hooks or sinkers on the lines when there's no extras in the tackle box." He folded his arms. "Come on. Talk to me. Why?"

"I don't know . . . I guess . . . well—"

"I can't hear you," Dad said.

"I guess, well, the tackle box is, like, my favorite toy, but it's not a toy. It's better." I shrugged again. "I didn't want to share it."

Dad kept staring at me. I let out a breath and tried one more time to explain.

"It was so new. Guess I wasn't ready to, you know, let anybody use it."

Now it was Dad's turn to let out a breath. He sat down and looked at me.

"Why didn't you say something?" he asked, softer now.

I shrugged again.

"Look, I think I can understand how you might've felt, now, but I'm no mind reader. You've got to speak up when something like this happens. Okay? You can't expect people to go around fishing for your feelings, you know."

He smiled a tiny smile. Fishing for your feelings. It was a joke, a little joke, an accidental joke, a dumb joke. But it was amazing how much better it made me feel.

"I'm real sorry," I said again, and I meant it.

Dad nodded and scratched his head.

"Well, if it's any consolation, I don't think the other kids even noticed," he said. "And the funny thing is, the stuff you put in sort of came in handy."

I looked up.

"Cyn hated fishing. She took one of the rags and made a headband and pretended she was some kind of karate kid. Teddy cut his thumb—I had to use another rag to bandage it up. Brad didn't much like fishing, either. He found a diaper and used it with his doll. Teddy even brought home the fish he caught in one of those big baggy socks you put in."

I almost asked if anyone found any use for the pairs of old underwear I had stuffed in, but I decided against it.

"What did you do with the five dollars I gave you?"

"I put it on your bureau." I spoke in a whisper.

"Didn't it feel strange taking the money?"

"Yeah."

"Then why did you?"

"I don't know. I was, like, in shock."

"Know what I want you to do?" Dad asked.

"What?" Here it comes, I thought: no allowance, grounded for a month, maybe worse.

"I want you to go upstairs and get that money. Take it and put it in your wallet. Find a special place for it. Don't spend it. Keep it so you won't forget this."

"Okay," I said. I thought: I'll never *ever* forget this. I turned to go.

"Wait." Dad handed me the tackle box. "You'd better take this."

Upstairs, Nate smirked when I walked into the room.

"Dad was wicked mad, right?" he asked.

I didn't say anything.

"You get in trouble?"

I said nothing.

"You grounded or what?"

"Not really. He didn't really punish me like that."

"You're kidding."

"I'm not kidding."

Nate gave me a disgusted look.

"You get away with everything," he said. He shook his head and sat down heavily on his bed. "Tell you one thing, I'm not giving back your baseball cards."

I put the tackle box on my bed, opened it, and pulled out a clump of rags, diapers, underwear. . . . When the tackle box was empty again I took the fishing gear out of the bottom drawer of my dresser and started putting it back into the little drawers where it belonged.

"You gave me your cards fair and square," Nate said. "No trade backs, right?"

I poured the sinkers into one of the little drawers. Nate kept staring at me, expecting me to say something.

"Do you want them back?" Nate asked. "Because—"

"Nope," I said. "I don't."

"I can keep them? Really?"

"Really. They're all yours."

It seemed like a small price to pay.

# 5. Traded Away

Late that summer, Cyn started acting funny. I first noticed it when Grandma Annie came for her summer visit. Grandma arrived with a box of chocolates for Mom and little presents for each of us kids, but mostly she arrived with blueberries on her mind. First chance she got she loaded up the car with a picnic lunch to go pick blueberries in Plymouth, Massachusetts. We always went to the same place: a forest where there had been a big fire a few years before.

"Burnt forests are bad news for Mother Nature but great news for blueberries," Grandma said. "No better place on earth for blueberrying."

She always handed out empty coffee cans (the kind with a snug-fitting plastic top) to hold the berries we picked. Soon as you took off the top a strong coffee smell rose up and tickled your nostrils.

It sure gave you a peculiar feeling to have that coffee smell spilling out in the middle of a burnt-out forest.

Grandma was a picking machine; she could easily outpick the rest of us kids combined. "Pick, don't eat!" she'd scold, but it was a pretend kind of scolding, half serious, half laugh. The little kids ate most of the berries they picked. For us older kids it was two berries in the can (plink! plink!), two in your mouth, two in the can, two in your mouth, until pretty soon your lips and tongue and teeth were stained such a dark blue that when Grandma asked, "Are you picking or *munching* those berries?" it didn't do any good trying to lie, not with a mouth gone all blue like that.

Grandma's summer visits meant blueberry everything: muffins, cakes, and turnovers. Best of all: pies. If you haven't tasted Grandma Annie's blueberry pie, warm, with a flaky crust, topped with a big scoop of goats' milk vanilla ice cream (homemade from the Gonsalveses' farm three streets away) melting streams of white into the dark blue filling, and felt in your mouth the delicious war between the warm pie and the cold ice cream, well, I feel awfully sorry for you. I really do.

"Coming blueberrying with us, Cynthia?" Grandma asked. We were in the kitchen gathering the empty coffee cans we'd need for picking.

"No, I'm not," Cyn replied. She folded her arms. "I think it's wrong."

"Wrong?" I asked. "Why?"

"All sorts of wild animals need those berries to live on," Cyn said. She peered at me, lips pressed together. "Ever consider that?"

Grandma looked surprised. We all did.

"What kind of wild animals?" Nate asked.

"Squirrels, turtles, lots of bird species!" Cyn said.

It bugged me to hear her use that word: *species*. Lately Cyn was starting to sound like a real know-it-all.

"Bears, too," Cyn was saying. "That's the problem with this world—nobody ever thinks about the animals."

"I seriously doubt there's any bears living out there," Nate put in.

"We can feed the animals," Brad told Cyn. "We'll give them bread and cookies."

"They need fresh fruit," Cyn told him.

"That's the craziest thing I've ever heard," I said. "I mean, there's a ton of berries in those woods."

"But it's wrong to pick *their* blueberries," Cyn said. "It's stealing. They need those berries to live on, to feed their young."

Nate stood up, bowed down to Cyn, and chanted: "Oh, Cyn, Oh Great Protector of Wild Animals."

"Go play in traffic!" Cyn told him.

"Hush, both of you!" Grandma put her arm around Cyn and pulled her against her. "Honey, don't you think there's enough berries to go around?"

"No." Cyn looked away. "I mean, there's nothing

wrong with people eating farm-grown berries. But wild blueberries should be left for wild animals."

"But you *always* pick blueberries with your grandma," Grandma said. "I'll miss you."

"You'll never change her mind," I said. "She's stubborn."

"I'm *right*," Cyn snapped.

So we went without Cyn and we picked a small mountain of berries; it was a toss-up between Teddy and Brad as to who had the bluest mouth. When we got home Grandma and Mom started in making pies, but Cyn wouldn't help. She boycotted the berries. As far as I could tell she didn't touch a single one.

Then it happened. The next week, right after Grandma left, Cyn traded families. No kidding. She traded us away. She traded our family the way you might trade away a not-so-special marble, or one of your baseball card doubles.

She traded us for the Wynns, the family that lived at the end of our street. The Wynns were Mrs. Wynn, a veterinarian, and Cyn's best friend, Sharon. Mr. Wynn, a high school music teacher, had died of a heart attack a few years before. "His heart attacked him" is how Brad put it, which wasn't meant to be funny though everybody laughed when Brad said it.

Cyn found the Wynns' small family superior to ours in almost every way: a house with millions of plants, tons of room, no pesty brothers, plus all kinds of rabbits, cats, dogs, and birds. Cyn spent every possible moment over there: after school, all day Saturday, most of Sunday. She ate dinner there every chance she got.

One day Mom stopped Cyn as she hurried through the kitchen to the back screen door.

"Where are you going?" Mom asked.

"Sharon's house," Cyn said. She glanced over at the stove and wrinkled her nose at the sight and smell of Mom browning hamburger for a spaghetti sauce. Ever since Cyn found out that the Wynns were vegetarians she had decided to go veggie, too. She stopped eating meat of any kind and let it be known that she disapproved when the rest of us ate "flesh food."

"When'll you be home?"

"Don't know."

"Please be home by five for supper."

"Oh, all right," Cyn said on her way out.

"She doesn't seem to like us very much," I said to Mom.

"Oh, I think she likes us," Mom said. "It's just a stage she's going through. She's starting to separate."

That made me laugh; all I could picture was Cyn's body breaking into pieces, and the pieces floating away in different directions. "What do you mean?"

"She's finding out who she really is," Mom explained. "So she's breaking away from us a little. It's a normal, healthy part of growing up. But it can be painful."

I didn't understand. Neither did anyone else.

A week later at dinner Brad asked Cyn: "You play with me?"

"Can't tonight," Cyn said. Brad was Cyn's favorite. Sometimes she called him The Little Prince.

"Why?"

"I'm going over to Sharon's tonight. Can I, Mom?"

"It's pretty late," Mom said.

"Tomorrow?" Brad asked, looking up.

"Okay." Cyn smiled at him. "Please, Mom."

"No, I think you better not."

"But I *have* to."

"Why?"

"To talk to Sharon."

"I'm sure you'll see her tomorrow morning bright and early," Mom said.

"Ever hear of the telephone?" Nate asked Cyn.

"Shut up," Cyn said.

"We don't use language like that in this house," Dad said.

"He's always bugging me." Cyn folded her arms.

"What's the *deal* with you and that family?" Nate asked.

"None of your business." Cyn looked away.

"You practically *live* over there," Nate said. "Why don't you change your last name to theirs? Cyn Wynn. Cyn Wynn. Hey, that rhymes!" He laughed.

"Mom!"

"Nathan. Please."

"Go chew that bloody piece of cow flesh," Cyn said, pointing at Nate's plate.

"Not a bad idea," Nate said. He put a big piece of steak into his mouth, closed his eyes, and chewed slowly. "Mmmmm."

"Disgusting," Cyn said. She got up and left the table.

Later Mom and Dad sat down with Nate and me.

"I don't like to hear that kind of teasing," Dad told Nate.

"But Dad, you gotta admit, it's pretty weird all the time she spends down there," Nate said. "She hardly ever hangs out around here."

"Try to understand what it must be like being the only girl in this family," Dad said. "Imagine being surrounded by two older sisters and three younger sisters. Don't you think it might make you a little crazy?"

Nate just shrugged.

"Sharon is like a sister for Cyn," Mom said. "This is a stage she just has to go through. You watch. She'll outgrow it."

But she didn't outgrow it. All summer Cyn and Sharon spent every possible moment together. They went to the same summer camp and took swimming lessons together. We hardly ever saw Cyn. When we did see her she'd usually be with Sharon and the two of them would be wearing the same kind of braids or barrettes or scarfs or headbands or dresses.

The Siamese Twins, Dad called them.

"It's like they share a brain," Nate muttered, and I kind of agreed.

The big event of the summer was Nate's junk sale. Nate had collected tons of stuff during his long walks through the woods and junkyards and building sites. Our basement held at least a dozen cardboard boxes filled with his junk. Nate loved taking apart anything mechanical; he had two big boxes filled with nothing but parts he'd taken from bikes, cars, and small engines. Mom finally got him to agree to get rid of it, or some of it at least. Nate decided he'd keep his very best junk and try to sell the rest.

I thought selling junk was a very weird idea, but I did help write out notices advertising the sale and spread the word around the neighborhood. Mom helped Nate label and price the junk. Dad and I carried two picnic tables (ours plus one borrowed from the Montgomerys next door) to the front yard. Brad and Teddy set up a stand to sell lemonade and cookies.

The sale started at ten o'clock. I honestly didn't expect anyone to show up, but by nine thirty kids were already starting to line up and at ten sharp at least a dozen kids were out there pawing through the boxes of Nate's stuff. They weren't just looking, either—these kids came to buy. They bought comic books, an old meat grinder, a rodeo spur, a snakeskin, a pair of dented cymbals, an old-fashioned balance scale, amethyst crystals. You never saw anything like it: they handed Nate cold cash in return for his prized junk. By lunchtime the cookies, the lemonade, and most of the junk were all gone and Nate had thirty bucks in his pocket.

Maybe it wasn't so much the junk itself that appealed to the kids as it was the fact that Nate owned it. People liked Nate, and when he collected something it became valuable. I wondered how long the spell would last. Those kids took Nate's junk home thinking it was the most incredible treasure on Earth, but pretty soon it would turn back into regular junk again.

That was the most exciting day of the summer, and I kept expecting to see Cyn, who was down at the Wynns' house playing with Sharon, as usual. But Cyn never showed.


Labor Day came and went. School started: Cyn and Sharon were put in the same class. One day Cyn came into the living room. All five boys—me, Nate, Teddy, Brad, and Josh—were on the floor watching TV. Dad was reading the newspaper. He looked up when he saw Cyn.

"Hey, stranger," he said, snatching her onto his lap. "My little Cyn-Bad, Cyn-Bad, Cyn-Bad the Sailor. Back home from your travels around the world?"

She gave him a sour look. Only Dad could fool around with her name. Everybody else had to call her Cyn.

"I'm not Sinbad," she told him. "I'm not a sailor. I don't like boats."

"No, you're my Cyn-derella, is what you are."

"Not Cinderella, either," she said quietly. "More like Snow White with the seven dwarfs."

"Snow White? You?" Nate snorted. "Yeah, you wish."

"Be quiet, dwarf," Cyn said, pointing at him.

"Ha!" Dad laughed and tickled her. She squirmed but didn't crack a smile.

"Can I spend Thanksgiving with the Wynns?" Cyn asked. "It's all right with Mrs. Wynn but she said I should ask you."

"Absolutely not," Dad said.

"Why not?"

"I want you here with us. No kidding, I'd miss you something terrible if you were gone on Thanksgiving."

"Can Sharon come *here* for Thanksgiving?"

"I don't think so," Dad said.

"Why not?"

"Thanksgiving is about family," Dad said. "It's prime family time."

"Well, I don't *want* this family," she shouted. She twisted out of his grip and stomped upstairs.

A couple weeks later while I was eating lunch in the dining room I overheard this conversation between Cyn and Mom.

Mom: "What do you two *do* together for so many hours?"

Cyn (softly): "Talk."

Mom: "About what?"

Cyn: "Stuff."

Mom: "What kind of stuff?"

Cyn: "All sorts of stuff. Wizards. Trolls. Magic stuff. We have lots of, like, pretend friends."

Mom: "Mmmmm."

Cyn: "Real things, too. Animals. I want to be a vet when I grow up. Like Mrs. Wynn."

Mom: "I think you'd make a wonderful vet."

Cyn: "Think we can have one of Cappuccino's kittens? Mrs. Wynn said I could have one if you give me permission."

Mom: "I don't think so."

Cyn: "Please? I'm dying for a kitten. I don't want anything else."

Mom: "I don't know. I don't think so."

Cyn: "Please, Mom."

Mom: "You know how your father is about pets. You'll have to talk it over with him."

Dad surprised everybody: he agreed. Cyn could get a kitten. Maybe he thought a kitten would keep her around our house more.

The next day we all went over to the Wynns' to see the kittens. The mother had short fur in patches of coffee with swatches of black and white. Two kittens were colored just like the mother, and three had solid-colored fur: one black, one white, and one whose fur was the color of a piece of caramel. The caramel one licked my thumb with a sandpapery tongue.

"How old are they?" Dad asked.

"Just eight weeks," Mrs. Wynn said. "Kittens should be anywhere from eight weeks to twelve weeks old before they get separated from the mother."

"Which one do you want?" Dad asked Cyn. I was hoping she'd say the caramel-colored one, but Cyn pointed at the white kitten in the corner of the box. She was sound asleep, her head buried in her tail.

"And she can come home and visit Cappuccino whenever she wants," Mrs. Wynn said. "She'll be right down the road."

"Lemme guess," Nate said to Cyn. "You're going to name the kitten . . . Salt? Marshmallow? Sugar!"

"Snow," Cyn told him.

"Just Snow?" Dad asked. "How about Snowflake? Or Snow White?"

"Snowball!" Teddy yelled.

"Snowball Fight," Brad said with a smile.

"Snow," Cyn said.

"How 'bout Snowball?" Nate said. "How 'bout Snowstorm?"

"Snow," Cyn said.

"Snowdrop," I suggested to Cyn. "Snowshoe."

"Snowshoe?" She gave me a funny look.

"Well, her feet are white," I said.

"How about Snowy?" Dad suggested.

"Her name is Snow," Cyn said. "Period."

Snow arrived at our house two days later. The house was quiet when Cyn carried in a cardboard box. Mom, Nate, and I followed her into the living room, where she set the box on the floor in front of the couch. Cyn gently lifted the kitten out of the box and cradled it in her lap.

"Welcome to your new home," she murmured.

"Isn't she beautiful," Mom said.

"She's so tiny," Nate said.

At that moment Teddy thundered into the room, waving his arms wildly, with Brad close behind. The sight of a real live kitten in our house put Teddy into a frenzy.

"HERE, KITTY! KITTY!" he yelled.

"Shh, you're scaring her!" Cyn said. The kitten shrank down beneath Cyn's hands.

"Step back," Mom told him.

"HERE, KITTY!" Teddy yelled. "LEMME HOLD IT!"

"Stop it!" Mom yelled, but Teddy lurched forward and Snow squirmed from Cyn's grasp. She bounded away in three quick jumps. You wouldn't think a tiny kitten could move that fast. Snow scampered behind the couch. Everybody scrunched down to look for her.

"Now look what you've done!" Cyn cried. In a softer voice she called: "Snow! Easy, Snow! Everything's going to be all right!"

"Where is it?" Teddy cried. He tried to rush forward, but Mom grabbed him and sat him next to her on the couch.

"Sit down!" she said. "You must use a softer voice around that kitten. Do you understand? She's scared. She's away from her mother for the first time, in a strange new place. How would you feel? You're not helping when you yell like that."

"I don't see her," Nate said.

"Pull back the couch," Cyn said. Mom and I pulled gently on one side but there was no kitten there.

"Snow!" Cyn called.

"Snow!" Teddy called, very softly. Cyn gave him a mean look.

"I could kill you!" she hissed at him.

"I'll help you find her," Teddy said.

"You'd better find her!"

We began searching the house. Nobody looked harder than Cyn or Teddy. We knew Snow was tiny enough to fit into the smallest spaces, so we even searched the toy chest, the shelves of the bookcases.

Mom, Cyn, and Teddy looked upstairs in the closets, under all the beds. Brad checked under the couches and behind the radiators. Nate and I checked every inch of the basement.

When Dad came home from work he got his flashlight and searched the crawl space under the stairs. But Snow wasn't under there, either.

"Could she have slipped outside?" he asked.

"I don't see how," I said. "Both doors were closed."

"Let's have some supper," Mom said. "We can look for Snow afterward."

"I'm going to keep looking," Cyn said, her lips clenched together. "I can't eat."

"Me, too," Teddy said, walking sadly behind her.

For dinner we had clam chowder, grilled cheese sandwiches, chips, and salad. I ate guiltily, watching Cyn and Teddy walk into this room or that, calling: "Snow! Snow! Here, kitty! Here, Snow!"

"She's gotta be here somewhere," Teddy kept saying. "She's gotta be."

Another hour passed. By now it was totally dark outside and we were all sitting in the living room. Cyn slouched on the couch saying nothing, doing nothing, and nothing anyone said could make her feel better. She had a look on her face as though someone had died.

"Sorry, Cyn," Teddy said. "I just wanted to hold her."

"I know," Cyn whispered without looking at him.

"It doesn't make sense," Nate said. "A kitten can't

just disappear into thin air. It's not scientifically possible."

"I still think we'll find her," Dad said. "And if we don't find Snow we can get another kitten. That light brown one looked awful cute."

"I don't want another one!" Cyn said, beginning to sniffle. "Doesn't anybody understand? I want Snow."

Nobody spoke. Then Teddy jumped up and stood as if frozen, staring at the fireplace. Slowly Cyn stood up beside him. Teddy rushed forward. He pulled down the screen surrounding the fireplace. A small dark creature jumped past him and stood, shivering, in the middle of the living room floor. It looked like a grayish rat. Cyn rushed forward to scoop it up.

"Snow!" Cyn cried. Everyone came closer. It *was* Snow, but the kitten had so much soot on her fur you never would have guessed she had once been white.

"I FOUND HER!" Teddy yelled.

"The chimney!" Mom said. "She was hiding in the chimney!"

"How do you like that?" Dad stood there, shaking his head.

"Oh, Cyn, look, you're getting soot all over your sweater!" Mom said. But Cyn didn't hear. She kept grinning and rocking back and forth, hugging the kitten, talking softly, her own face covered with dark streaks of soot.

"Hiding in the chimney!" Brad cried, jumping up and down.

"Why didn't I think of that?" I said.

"I FOUND HER!" Teddy cried again. "I saw these little eyes blinking at me behind the screen!"

"Yes, you did," Mom said, squeezing him. "Eagle eyes strikes again! Cyn: Snow is going to need a bath. And so are you!"

"The chimney!" Dad kept saying over and over. "The chimney, of all places! How do you like that?"

"Isn't she *smart*?" Cyn asked, hugging the kitten and grinning up with her filthy face.

# 6. The Headless Chicks

The last Saturday in September Uncle Billy stopped in for a visit. He brought four big red helium balloons; Brad and I took them to a far corner of the backyard, the place farthest away from the house. While we were out there we came up with a strange idea: we would take acorns, hollow them out, and insert a small piece of paper with a message in each one. We planned to attach the acorns to the balloons and send them all up into the air.

"We could even put ants in with the message!" I said. "They can be like little astronauts!"

"No," Brad said, eyes narrowed. "They'd be scared to be up so high. And it would be hard for them to breathe."

"True," I admitted. "But what should I write? For the message?"

"I don't know," Brad said, holding the balloons by

the ends of their strings and bouncing up and down from excitement. It was a warm Indian summer day. He was dressed in shorts and had bare feet. "Depends on who's going to read it, I guess."

"Who do *you* think'll read it?"

"Well, if the balloons go into outer space, space creatures might read it," he said seriously. "Aliens."

"You really think so?" I swiveled around to look at him. Brad's eyes were light brown, like mine. We had the same build, much leaner than either Nate or Teddy. When you looked at Brad you couldn't help noticing his eyebrows, which were thick and darker brown than his hair and made an unbroken line across his lower forehead. As I looked at him, a word entered my mind and the word was *gullible*.

"Nate says the Ramseys are aliens," Brad whispered, as if someone might overhear. "He says you can tell because they all have such big heads. He says they're from Saturn or Neptune, he's not sure."

I laughed. The Ramseys had moved into the neighborhood the year before. There were three boys, all quiet kids who hardly ever left their yard. They all wore crewcuts and, come to think of it, their heads were unusually large.

"The Ramseys aren't aliens!" I told him. "Nate's just pulling your leg!"

He looked at me, surprised.

"He's teasing you," I told him.

Brad lowered his eyes.

"He always does that," Brad said, suddenly glum.

He came and sat beside me, pulling the balloons down with him. "He tells me some story and I always believe it's true."

"You ought to get back at him," I said. "Figure out some way to play a joke on him. Give him a dose of his own medicine. But, hey, we gotta write these messages. How about something like: *Whoever finds these—*"

A loud scream from the front yard. A few seconds later Nate appeared.

"Come quick!" he yelled. "It's Uncle Billy!"

I beat Brad to the front yard and found Uncle Billy lying on the grass, belly-up, absolutely motionless. Nate was standing beside him.

"He's dead!" Nate said with a quick glance at me. Brad looked up at me, too. I stared back at Nate, hesitated a moment, and decided to go along with it. For now.

"How'd it happen?" I asked in a shocked whisper.

"Heart failure," Nate said. "Uncle Billy always complained he had a bad ticker." He spoke as if he was talking about a leak in some pipe.

"Dead?" Brad asked. He was still holding the four red balloons.

"As a doornail," Nate replied. "Take a good look at him."

We looked down at Uncle Billy lying on the grass, facing the sky. His eyes were closed, the muscles in his face slack and still. His arms and legs were sprawled out where he'd fallen. His hair was mussed.

I knelt down and put my ear to his mouth. No breath.

"Uncle Billy?" Brad asked. "Can't be." He looked dazed—his upper lip trembled.

"Watch this," Nate replied. He sprinkled blades of grass on Uncle Billy's face. Nothing. Then he dropped several small twigs; they bounced off Uncle Billy's cheeks and forehead as if were a statue.

"He's dead," Brad wailed. "Mom, c'mere! Uncle Billy's dead!"

The panic in Brad's voice made me uneasy. Maybe we had gone too far. Cyn ran outside to see what the fuss was all about.

"Uncle Billy's dead!" Brad said to Cyn, pointing down. "He's dead!"

"Dead?" Cyn gave Nate a disgusted look and patted Brad on the top of his head. She hated when anyone teased him. "Ha! If he's dead then I'm the queen of England."

Brad looked at her hopefully. Cyn took a long piece of grass and started tickling Uncle Billy under his chin. He didn't move.

"WAKE UP!" she practically yelled in his ear. Still nothing. She balanced an acorn on Uncle Billy's forehead.

"I KNOW YOU'RE NOT DEAD!" she yelled again, but he didn't move. Finally Brad couldn't stop himself; he let out a choking sob.

"Isn't it sad?" Nate said. "He was such a nice old man!"

"ARGHH!" Uncle Billy leaped up, lunged at Nate,

and began chasing him around the yard. That made Brad jump so much he lost hold of the balloons and they started rising away from him. Seeing the balloons floating up, he began to laugh and yell—"Come back!"—while Uncle Billy caught Nate, grabbed him by the wrists, and swung him around and around until Nate was so dizzy and weak from laughter he couldn't even stand. Finally we all collapsed on the grass.

"Fooled you!" Nate said to Brad. "Again!"

"I don't care," Brad replied, shrugging. "I'm *glad* it was a joke."

"Don't believe everything you see," Uncle Billy told Brad.

"Where'd you learn to play dead so good?" I asked him.

"In the war," he replied. "Playing dead kept me alive more than once, lemme tell you. One time—"

Just then Teddy poked his head out of the kitchen door.

"COME QUICK! IT'S JOSH!"

We raced inside. Josh was sitting in front of the refrigerator, grinning like a madman, with grease all over his face. In his right hand there was the silvery wrapper from a stick of butter.

"JOSH GOT INTO THE BUTTER!" Teddy cried.

"Butter good!" Josh said. "Mmmmmmm."

"My God!" Nate yelled. "What? He—oh no—the kid ate a STICK OF BUTTER! A WHOLE STICK OF BUTTER! Gross!"

"I think I'm going to be sick," Cyn said. She sat down and covered her eyes.

"Holy canary," Uncle Billy said, shaking his head. "We got ourselves a butterball turkey here, and it's not even Thanksgiving!"

"BUTTER MONSTER!" Teddy yelled. He screamed with laughter.

"It's not funny," I said. "This could be serious."

"Yeah," Brad said. He yelled, "Mom, come down here, quick!"

"That's so disgusting!" Nate said, holding his stomach. "I'm gonna puke! A SOLID STICK OF BUTTER? I mean, it's PURE RAW FAT!"

"Did you?" I asked Josh. "Did you eat a whole stick of butter?"

"Butter good," Josh replied seriously.

"No, Josh," Brad said. "Too much butter is bad."

"Butter can make you fat," Uncle Billy told him. "Better watch out. Do you want to be the fat man at the circus?"

To this question Josh nodded seriously, yes, which cracked everybody up. Mom came into the room and looked down at Josh.

"He ate it, Mom!" Nate said. "A stick of butter! Can you believe it? Should we take him to the hospital and get his stomach pumped out?"

"Shh," Mom said, squatting down in front of Josh. She took the butter wrapper from him and wiped some grease off his face. "What's gotten into you,

you little monkey? You don't eat a stick of butter like you eat a Popsicle!"

"Butter good," Josh said, licking his lips.

"A little butter is perfectly fine," she told him, "but too much butter might make a little boy sick!"


That night, in honor of Josh not having to get his stomach pumped, Uncle Billy opened a package of Peeps, those marshmallow chicks that are coated in yellow sugar. Before dinner he put one marshmallow chick on each person's plate. Soon after that Dad called everyone to supper. The moment we raced into the dining room Nate gasped. He stared down at his plate, a look of pure horror on his face. His expression made me look down, too. Someone had bitten off my chick's head! There was a headless chick sitting on my plate!

"The head's gone!" Cyn cried.

"Mine, too!" Nate yelled. We glanced around the table. On every plate the same thing: someone had bitten the heads off *all* the marshmallow chicks.

"All right, who did it?" Teddy demanded.

"Yeah, like you didn't know!" Nate said to Teddy.

"I DIDN'T!" Teddy yelled.

"Shhh!" Mom told him.

"Yeah, right," Nate said to Teddy.

"Uncle Billy, did you have anything to do with this?" Cyn asked suspiciously.

"Nope, cross my heart," Uncle Billy said, raising both hands.

"We got ourselves a mystery," Dad said, leaning down so he could take a careful look at his own headless chick.

Just then I noticed Brad sitting very quietly in his seat, trying to look normal. Trying to look innocent. With a small but unmistakable smear of yellow sugar just above his upper lip.

"Brad, do you know anything about this?" Dad asked.

Everybody stared at Brad. Brad grinned.

"I did it," he said.

I kept staring at him. Brad was the last person in the family you'd expect to pull a stunt like this. Dad and Mom just looked at each other.

"Why on earth would you do such a thing?" Mom asked. She seemed more surprised than mad.

"To get back at Nate for always pulling my leg," Brad said, grinning.

"You decapitated my chick!" Nate yelled, scowling at Brad.

"Yeah, I started with yours," Brad said with a giggle, "and it tasted so good I just kept on going."

Teddy was the first one who started to laugh. He laughed so hard he almost started choking and he had to drink some water to calm down.

# 7. A Steaming Bowl
# of Sadness

It happened on October 15. At four thirty-five in the afternoon the phone rang at our house. Brad, who was eight, had been riding his bike, tearing down a hill with a bunch of other kids and talking to his best friend, Jack Wells, at the same time. The way we heard it, Brad turned his head and smashed full speed into an ambulance parked on the street.

Somebody found the ambulance driver. He rushed Brad, who was unconscious, to Good Samaritan Hospital.

Mom was in the kitchen slicing up Greek olives for a special olive-feta-cheese-and-sun-dried-tomato-over-pasta dish she made, Dad's favorite supper. The phone rang. When Mom hung up she put Josh in his car seat and drove straight to Good Sam. I came, too, and I'd never known Mom to drive so fast. We met Dr.

Wentworth in the intensive care waiting room. He stood there wringing his big hands. Shaking his head. Avoiding our eyes.

"It's very, very bad," Dr. Wentworth said. "His brain stem—he practically severed it."

"Brain stem?" Mom asked.

"The part at the lower back of the head. It connects the brain to the top of the spine. It's . . ." He shook his head.

"What? What does it mean?"

For the first time he looked at her.

"Well?" she demanded.

He spoke in a croaking whisper. "There's really no hope, Lisa."

Mom stepped back, as if someone or something had just struck her in the face.

"I can't accept that," she said.

In the waiting room Josh met a little girl with flaming red hair, and they had a terrific time playing with fire trucks. After a while Dad came to the hospital with Mrs. Wynn; she was there to take me and Josh back home.

When we got back to our house we found the kids in the living room: Nate watching TV, Teddy coloring, Cyn reading with Snow curled up on her lap. They all stopped what they were doing and looked up.

"Uncle Billy's here," Teddy said. "Brad okay?"

"No, he's hurt real real bad," I told him. Teddy lowered his head.

I found Uncle Billy in the kitchen with two neighbors, Mrs. McDonough and Mr. Hunt. Mrs. McDonough was holding what looked like a casserole; Mr. Hunt stood next to a plate of cold cuts on the table. There was food all over the place: bread, pasta salad, pizza, homemade cookies, a cake, soda, and juice.

"Cliff." Uncle Billy gave me a quick hug. "How is he?"

"I don't know, I didn't see him," I said, trying to control the quaver in my voice. "But Dr. Wentworth says he's hurt real bad."

"We're sorry about your brother," Mr. Hunt said, nodding and edging toward the door.

"We're all praying for him," Mrs. McDonough said. Then, to Uncle Billy, "Call if there's anything I can do. I mean it. Anything at all." She and Mr. Hunt left.

For supper we ate the pizza somebody brought over. The meal was interrupted at least a dozen times by the phone ringing—relatives, mostly, wanting to know about Brad. Uncle Billy answered the phone and kept the calls short.

"We're waiting to hear from the hospital," he said each time. "I've got to keep this line free."

Dad called and talked to Uncle Billy for a few minutes.

"There's no change," Uncle Billy said after he hung up.

No hope.

After supper I gave Josh his bath and then read him his bedtime stories—that helped keep my mind away from the hospital. Everyone else was quiet.

Even Teddy just sat around watching TV. Uncle Billy let me and Nate stay up past our bedtimes. I half expected Cyn and Teddy to ask to stay up late, too, but they headed off to bed without a word.

Nate and I sat in the living room with Uncle Billy, watching a football game on TV and drinking cocoa. Nate kept fiddling with this little cloth bag filled with ball bearings he'd pulled out of an abandoned refrigerator. We were all pretty jumpy, and by ten o'clock the muffled metallic click-click-clicks were driving me crazy.

"Will you stop that?" I asked him.

Uncle Billy made popcorn. We watched more TV. At eleven Nate and I couldn't stay awake any longer. We said good night to Uncle Billy and went to bed.

During the night the bedroom door opened. I opened my eyes and smelled, before I saw, my mother. The light snapped on. Dad and Mom. Dad sat on my bed. On the other side of the room Nate sat up in bed, blinking. I watched Mom bend down to pick up a dirty sock Nate had left on the rug.

"Brad died about a half hour ago," Dad said.

He looked at me, waiting. His face looked old. I turned away and watched Mom bend down and pick up another dirty sock. Her face was stone.

"We were with him when he died," Dad said.

I tried to speak, but nothing came out.

Mom stood there, looking down at the rug. There were no more dirty socks to pick up, so she knelt down and started picking up tiny bits of lint.

Dad said, "We thought you two should be the first to know."

"I don't want to hear any more about it," Nate said, turning away. "I just don't." He made a small sound, like a whimper, then nothing.

Dad touched my shoulder. He went to the other bed and put his hand on Nate's back. He left the room. Mom turned to look at me.

"I think he knew we were there," she said. She turned off the light and closed the door behind her.

About a million things happened after that, though most of it got blurry and didn't stick in my mind. What did stick were odd things, little details you'd think shouldn't have mattered but somehow did.

Like something I overhead this kid at the funeral home (there were dozens of kids Brad's age) saying to another kid: "He never even made it to double digits." *Double digits*: for some reason those words kept bouncing around in my head.

Like my Aunt Joan getting mad at my cousin Fred for not wearing a tie to the wake.

Like Mom looking for Brad's favorite shirt to bury him in, a soccer shirt from Brazil with a picture of

Pelé on the front that Uncle Billy once gave him. She finally found the shirt but it was dirty, and she washed it so he could be buried in a clean shirt.

Like the great debate among relatives as to whether or not Grandma Annie should be told about Brad's death. I thought it was stupid: of *course* she should be told, though Aunt Pat argued that the news might be "too much" for someone her age. Finally they did tell Grandma and Uncle Billy drove her to the funeral.

"Not right," she said later at our house. A mound of used tissues had grown up on the table beside her. "He should be here crying at *my* funeral. It's not right. Here I am past eighty. It's my time, not his."

"We wouldn't want that, Mom," Mom said through her own tears.

The funeral. The church jam-packed. All that sniffling and sobbing and nose blowing.

Teddy tucked his head under my mother's arm. He and Mom cried nonstop.

Cyn cried quietly. No sobs or noise, just silent streams running down her face. I guess she was about as close to Brad as anyone.

Nobody really explained to Josh about Brad, I guess because they figured he wouldn't understand. But somehow he did understand, at least enough so that he cried, and Dad had to hold him through the service.

Even Dad cried a little.

Nate stood dry-eyed and still. His jaw was set, as though he was biting something hard.

I couldn't cry, either. I tried, and wondered: What's wrong with me? During the funeral I stared hard at the candles, thinking that might start some tears, but it didn't work. Only later at the cemetery when they started lowering his coffin down into the ground and it hit me that this wasn't some bad dream, that we were really going to lose Brad forever, did I feel some water come into my eyes. But it dried up faster than dew under hot sun.

After the funeral everyone came back to our house to eat and drink. I really wanted to get out of there, and I was thankful when Uncle Billy asked if I wanted to go for a drive.

We didn't talk in the car, but I could tell we were heading for the beach. The parking lot was practically empty. We parked, got out, and walked down to the water's edge. It was clear and pretty cold. We just walked along. For a couple minutes neither one of us said anything.

Then: "When I was in the navy they issued a pair of blue jeans to each of us. They were nice pants, you know, strong and well made, but stiff as a board. Uncomfortable? I guess they were."

He paused. Please, not another make-believe story, I was thinking, but I held my tongue.

"You know what we did?" Uncle Billy asked. "We used to tie the jeans to thick ropes, throw the ropes overboard, and drag the jeans through cold seawater.

We were probably breaking a hundred navy regulations, but we did it. We dragged our jeans through the Pacific Ocean for days on end. Then we pulled them in and threw them into the wash. Now they were soft, really comfortable to wear. Thing was, you couldn't leave them in the water too long. Four days, five days was about right. One guy left his jeans on the rope for seven days, and you know what happened? When he pulled them in they were all ripped to pieces."

He smiled at me.

"I guess I don't understand," I said.

Uncle Billy picked up a rock and skimmed it—three jumps—across the water.

"I don't know. The last couple days I've felt a little like those blue jeans must've felt, dragged through the ocean, night and day." He sighed. "Something like this really softens you up. But you can't let it break you apart, either."

I thought about that. I asked, "Think there's something wrong with me—that I haven't cried?"

"Hell, no!" He let out a short laugh. "During the war the hospitals had certain guys they called 'walking wounded.' These were men who had been through combat, but they looked fine, most of them. They could walk around, eat, and talk pretty regular. Didn't look like there was anything wrong with them, and there wasn't anything wrong—on the outside. But on the inside they were all twisted up. Their thoughts, feelings. They couldn't function. I knew guys like that." He took a deep breath. "Now that Brad's been taken from us I guess we're all walking wounded: you, me, all of us."

I nodded.

"Everybody reacts different to something like this—some people cry buckets, other folks store it up inside. When someone you love dies, you get a big bowl of sadness put down in front of you, steaming hot. You can start eating now, or you can let it cool and eat it bit by bit later on. Either way, you end up eating the whole thing. There's really no way around it."

For a while we had tons of flowers around the house (cut stems: severed brain stem) and lots of extra food until finally the flowers all wilted and the food got all eaten or spoiled, and then it was just our family again.

Teddy kept crying at night. He'd been used to sleeping with Brad and he didn't like sleeping in his bedroom alone. Cyn let him move into her bedroom. Dad said he'd turn Teddy and Brad's bedroom into an office. But for a while it stayed empty.

At school certain kids treated me differently. They kept their distance; they looked at me with funny eyes.

Truth is, I didn't know how to act, either. Only once before had someone I knew died: Bob Chidsey, my friend Chip's dad. I used to go over to Chip's house after school and around three thirty Mr. Chidsey would come downstairs, eyes all puffy with sleep. He worked the night shift as a security guard. A nice man, shy but friendly. He'd make us the most delicious crabmeat sandwiches: for some reason he always sliced off the crusts so all we ate was crabmeat with the nice soft inside bread. Then one day he went fishing and fell off his boat and hit his head and drowned. John Touse's big brother found the body, and for the next couple weeks Chip came to school with his eyes all puffy and red and I found myself keeping away from him in class. I didn't mean to, but I just didn't know what to say.

On the first of December I went down to the basement to see how the Christmas cactus was doing. It was doing exactly nothing. Mom brought it upstairs, but two weeks later it still didn't show any signs of waking up for Christmas. I phoned Grandma Annie.

"The cactus isn't blossoming at all," I told her. "It's not even budded."

She didn't answer, and I thought I heard a quiet sniffle.

"I wondered about that," she said. "Given what happened, I suspect it might not bud at all this year."

"Is it going to die, too?" I whispered.

"No," she sighed. "No, it'll come back. Just give it time."

# 8. Walking Wounded

It got closer to Christmas, but you wouldn't have known it from our house. No big wreath on the door. No mistletoe or candy canes or smiling Santas.

"Sharon asked why our house isn't decorated," Cyn said at dinner one night.

Dad looked up, over at Mom, then back at Cyn.

"What did you tell her?" he asked.

"I said we're not celebrating Christmas this year," she said softly.

"No Christmas this year," Nate said.

"I *want* Christmas," Josh said with panicky eyes.

"Well, you can't have Christmas." Nate gave him a stern look. "No Santa Claus this year. No presents either."

"I want *Christmas*," Josh said, starting to cry. His sobs filled the kitchen. Cyn glared at Nate.

"Proud of yourself?" she asked him.

"He just doesn't get it," Nate muttered.

"He's three years old," Mom said gently.

"I want you all to listen." Dad put down his fork. "This has been a very hard time. For everyone. And it's not going to get any easier anytime soon. Christmas won't be much fun. We're all in pain."

Across the table Nate rolled his eyes at me.

"We're just going to have to do the best we can," Dad said. "Mom and I have been thinking maybe this year we should do something different for Christmas. Maybe go away."

Pause. Josh wiped his nose on his sleeve.

"Where to?" Cyn asked.

"We thought we'd go to Vermont for a couple days," Dad said. "There's an inn up there that's supposed to be nice. We can skate, ski. There's a pool."

Nobody said anything.

"You can make your own sundaes at the restaurant," Dad said, smiling. "All the sundaes you can eat."

"Sundaes!" Josh grinned.

"We'll spend Christmas together," Dad said, "the best we can, and then come home."

"Will Grandma Annie come?" Teddy asked.

"No." Mom smiled at him. "Not this year. This year it'll be just us."

"We will have Christmas this year," Dad said, patting Josh's head. "But it will be a small Christmas."

"Yeah, so small you can't hardly see it," Nate said.

"What's wrong with you?" Dad asked him.

"Nothing's wrong," he said, folding his arms and looking away. "Everything's just great."

After dinner Dad asked Nate, Cyn, and me to stay in the kitchen.

"Christmas will be different this year," Dad said. "Your mother and I are trying to figure out what we should do about giving presents. What do you think?"

"I don't know," I said. Presents were the very last thing on my mind.

"I don't need anything," Nate said, tight-lipped.

Cyn said nothing.

"We were thinking it might be nice to do something small," Mom said after a moment. "Especially for Josh. Maybe we could just hang the stockings."

"Stockings," Dad repeated. "What do you guys think?"

"Okay by me." I shrugged. Really, I didn't care.

"That's good," Cyn said in a small voice.

"Great," Nate said. He didn't look at anybody.

We left the table, but Mom called me back.

"What are we going to do about Nate?" she asked. "I've never seen him so angry."

"I don't know, I really don't know," I said. Walking wounded, I kept thinking. I didn't want to be the oldest. For once I didn't want to think about taking care of the other kids. I couldn't. It was hard enough taking care of me.

On December 23 we packed the car, dropped Snow off at the Wynns' house, and started driving· to Vermont. It was snowing hard when we left, but the weather reports said the snow would turn to rain around midday. Dad drove leaning forward, all the while fiddling with the radio to find the latest news on the storm. Cyn and Mom sat next to him. Nate, Teddy, Josh, and I were in the back.

"Hey, gimme the crackers," Teddy said to Nate. "You gotta share."

"I haven't had hardly any," Nate told him.

"Gimme them, Piggie," Teddy said, trying to grab the box.

"You should talk." Nate snickered. "Had a look at your own belly lately?"

"Shut up, Big Mouth," Teddy shot back.

"This little piggie went to market—" Nate said.

"I know you are but what am I?"

"A pig."

"I know *you* are but—"

"Stop it!" Mom whirled around in the front seat. "Nate, Teddy, you two should be ashamed of yourselves. You're both old enough to know better."

Nate waited until she turned back around. Then he leaned forward and mouthed silently to Teddy: "Piggie!"

"Mom, Nate just called me Piggie again!"

"Liar!" Nate shouted with a loud laugh. "Didn't say a word."

"Hey." I tapped Nate on the shoulder. I spoke in a very soft whisper so that no one else could hear. "You're mad about Brad, okay, but don't take it out on him."

"What do *you* know?" Nate whispered back. "Why don't you write a little poem about it like that poem you wrote in school?

"Roses are red,
Violets are blue,
My brother is dead,
Boo hoo hoo hoo."

I stared at him. "I don't believe you," I said.

"Oh, shut up," Nate said in a bored voice.

"When are we gonna get there, Dad?" Cyn asked.

"A couple hours."

Josh looked up at me.

"Santa Claus gonna come," he said softly. "Santa Claus gonna bring me presents."


The snow never did turn to rain, and we didn't arrive at the Green Mountain Lodge until six o'clock, an hour and a half later than Dad had planned. It was a huge building, built in the 1800s, according to Dad, with a circular driveway and an antique horse carriage in front, painted black. The enormous red front door had a big white wreath on it, and white candles burned in all the windows.

"What do you think?" Dad asked.

"It looks lovely," Mom said.

"Sort of pretty," Cyn said.

Inside it was cozy, warm, and quiet except for the crackle of a big fire. The fire smell was mixed with the strong scent of cinnamon.

"Welcome!" the man at the front desk said. He motioned to a steaming pot at the table nearby. "Please help yourself to some hot apple cider while you warm up."

"Any kids here?" Nate asked the man.

"Nate!" Mom said. "Remember your manners."

"Well, as a matter of fact, there are lots of children staying here," the man said, smiling at Nate. "They're all in the restaurant right now. We start serving dinner at six."

"Great, I'm starved!" Dad said, rubbing his hands together.

Dad wasn't big on spending money. I figured he'd get two rooms, one for him and Mom and Cyn, and another for us four boys to jam into. But he got three rooms, one for him and Mom and Josh, one for Teddy and Cyn, one for Nate and me.

After dinner Mom and Dad went to the rec room with Cyn, Teddy, and Josh. Nate and I stayed in our room. He read Spiderman comics while he fiddled with that bag of ball bearings. Clickety-click-click-

click. I watched TV. At ten o'clock Mom came in to say good night and switch off the light. For a while I could feel Nate twitching and moving on the other side of the double bed.

"What're you thinking about?" I asked.

"Nothing much," he said.

"Wish we were home for Christmas?"

Nate said nothing.

"I do, sort of," I said.

"I wish Christmas were over and done with," Nate said, turning away from me.

Next morning at breakfast the little kids were excited. Christmas Eve. Through the tall windows in the dining room we could see a heavy snow falling. The night before, Teddy had made friends with three other boys. They had big plans for the day: making snow forts, hunting polar bears and woolly mammoths. Teddy gulped down his pancakes and ran off to join his new friends. He took two steps, then stopped and turned around.

"Is it okay, Mom?" he asked uncertainly.

"Go on," Mom said. "Have fun." Teddy smiled and ran off.

Watching him I felt amazed, annoyed.

"I'm glad someone's having fun around here," Dad said as he sipped his coffee.

"He acts like nothing's different," I said. "Weird."

"Well, it is a holiday," Mom said. She reached out

and gave my ribs a hard tickle. "Seems like it should be legal to have a tiny bit of fun. Huh, Nathan?"

Nate grunted without looking at her.

"We're doing the stockings tonight?" Cyn asked.

"We'll do what we always do," Mom said. "We'll hang them tonight and open them tomorrow morning."

"I was thinking," Cyn said.

"Oh no," Nate put up his hands in mock dread.

Ignoring him, Cyn said: "I think we should hang a stocking for Brad."

Silence. For five full seconds nobody moved.

"That's really dumb," Nate said.

"Nate," Dad said. "Please. Be quiet and listen."

"It's *dumb*," Nate repeated. "It is."

"*You* should talk about *dumb*," Cyn said, flashing him an icy look.

"What are you thinking?" Dad asked her.

Cyn looked down. "I had this present I was going to give him this year and . . . I . . . wanted to be able to put it into his stocking."

"That's fine," Dad said. He gave her a serious smile.

Mom nodded without speaking, a misty glaze in her eyes. I sat there hoping she wouldn't cry. She cried at almost anything these days. At least five times in the past couple months I'd come home from school and found Mom sobbing, going through the clothes in Brad's bureau. It made me think back to this game she used to play with me when I was little. When I got grumpy she'd go looking for my smile in the toy chest, under the bed, behind the radiator. A silly game but it worked; she got me looking, too, and somehow we always managed to find my smile in the end. Now she reached over and took Cyn's hand.

"I think that's a fine idea," Mom said softly.

Nate just shook his head.


The day passed slowly. Our family scattered in different directions. Dad took the little kids sledding. Mom and Cyn went ice-skating. I played video games and, later, took a walk through the snow to the horse barns. In the afternoon Mom and Dad took the little kids to the pool. I drank hot chocolate and played Ping-Pong with this older kid from New York City. He beat me badly, five games in a row. Tell you the truth, I didn't care.

Nate disappeared in the afternoon. He didn't show up again until five o'clock, and by then Mom and Dad had started to worry. Nate staggered into the inn, his clothes caked with snow, face white with cold.

"Where'd you go?" Dad asked with a tight smile. "We were starting to think about sending out the Saint Bernards."

"Took a long walk," Nate said. His mouth seemed frozen, too: the words came out funny. "Went farther than I've ever gone."

"Well, I'm glad you made it back!" Mom said. "Go

upstairs and get out of those wet things. I want you to take a nice hot bath before dinner."

That night they had planned a special sing-along by the huge fireplace. At dinner Mom asked if we wanted to come.

"Dad and I are taking Josh," she said.

"And me," Teddy said.

"I'll come," Cyn said carefully. "For a little while."

"If it's all right with you, I think I'd rather skip it," I told Mom.

"Ditto," Nate said.

Nate and I went upstairs to our room. He turned on the TV, but there were Christmas specials on practically every channel; you couldn't escape it. He did manage to find one old cowboy movie, and for a while we watched it without speaking. I kept expecting Mom and Dad to come back, but they didn't, and finally we were both bleary-eyed and yawning and Nate turned off the light.

After a minute, he sat up. Snapped the light on.

"Can you still remember what he looked like?" Nate asked.

"Who?" I looked at him.

"Who do you think? Brad, of course."

"Yeah, I think so," I said.

"Funny, but I can't picture his face."

"Well, don't worry," I said with a short laugh. "Dad

and Mom only have a couple million pictures of him."

"Remember the time that kid was picking on Brad?" Nate said. "At Brant Rock, long time ago. You remember that?"

"Yeah." There had been a tough kid, Ross McNally, who kept calling Brad "Brat" and laughing at him.

"He just couldn't do it," Nate said. "He kept trying to tease him, but Brad just stood there giving him one of those looks of his until Ross finally got mad and split."

"Brad could do that." I sat up. "He could look right through you. He was different. Remember the time he lost his first tooth? The tooth fairy left him four quarters, and he was so excited because he totally believed in the tooth fairy. But then Mom asked Brad if she could borrow the quarters and he got this really sad face. 'What's wrong?' she asked him and he said: 'You can't borrow this money. This is special money. This is *fairy money*.'"

"Fairy money!" That cracked Nate up. He bent over, banged his knee with his fists. I'd never seen him laugh so hard, but all of a sudden his face turned red, his shoulders quaked, and I realized he was crying.

I just sat there while he cried. If this had been a TV show, or a bad movie, I would've reached over and put my arm around him, comforted him. But this was no movie; this was real life. I knew Nate as well as I

119

knew anybody, and I knew the last thing he'd want was me putting my arm around him at a time like this. Nate would want to cry alone. And I let him. I went into the bathroom and got a bunch of tissues and put them on the bed beside him.

"Hey," I said. "How about when he bit the heads off all those marshmallow chicks? He really got you that time!"

"Yeah," Nate said. He let out a laugh, then lowered his head and began crying some more. Then he sat up and loudly blew his nose. Took a deep breath.

"This is really weird," he said.

"Yeah."

"You know, he used to say funny things, right?" Nate said. "Remember when he got scared of masks?"

"Oh, yeah." I remembered that. For two years any mask terrified Brad so much he wouldn't leave the house on Halloween.

"One time when he was little, around two or three, he was showing me the crawl space in the basement and he said, 'It's spooky down there. And it's *masky*!'" Nate laughed.

"Remember the night he saw Santa Claus?"

"Yeah! I mean, I believed he really did see Santa!"

"I *still* believe it!" I said.

Nate blew his nose again. "I just wish I could picture his face a little clearer," he said. "I do remember his eyes. Bright brown."

"Yeah, with yellowish streaks. He was a cute baby. Mom says people would stop on the street and make fools of themselves practically drooling all over him, but I forget that."

"That's just it—I don't want to forget," Nate said. He grabbed both of his ears and began crying some more.

A knock at the door. Dad came in.

"Hi, guys," he said. He sat on the bed and took a long look at our faces. "You two been watching a sad movie?"

"Something like that," I said.

Dad looked at Nate.

"You all right?"

"It's just not like Brad," Nate said, the words spilling out of him fast and high-pitched, louder and louder. "It's not like Brad, I mean, of all the stupid dumb idiotic freaking things for a kid to do, to smash into an ambulance! So stupid, Dad! So freaking stupid!"

He burst into tears again.

"I know," Dad said.

"I mean, what good are your eyes if you don't use them?" Nate sobbed. "Why didn't he look? Why didn't he open his eyes and *look*?"

"I know," Dad said. "I know."


A few minutes later everybody gathered in Mom

and Dad's room. It had a huge bed and a fireplace that worked. The stockings were hanging by the fireplace, already lumpy with little presents. My eyes flew to my blue-and-white stocking that Dad had borrowed to hang where Brad's used to be. I tucked a rolled-up piece of paper tied with ribbon into the stocking.

Cyn stood in front of Brad's stocking, holding something small.

"What is it?" Mom whispered. "Can you tell us what it is?"

Cyn opened her hand so we could see a chunk of beach glass. It was a beautiful piece, pale blue and deeply worn, about the size of a half-dollar. "I spent all last summer looking for a big blue piece. Remember? I didn't find it until the last day."

She put it into the stocking. Dad lifted the little kids, first Josh, then Teddy, so they could put their presents into Brad's stocking. Nate went up and dumped the whole bag of ball bearings into it. He went over and stood next to Mom.

"It's so dumb, Mom," Nate said, crying and sort of crumpling against her. "So unbelievably dumb."

"You're right," she said, hugging him. She closed her eyes and started to cry herself. For a while I think everyone was crying.

"Merry Christmas, everyone!" Dad said, wiping his eyes.

"Clifford," Mom said. She spoke to Dad. "This is a

nice enough place, but please, let's never, ever, come here again! Will you promise me that?"

"Promise," Dad said.


Nate and I went back to our bedroom and got into bed.

"What did you put in his stocking?" Nate asked me.

"A blank sheet of paper," I said. "I tried to write something but I just couldn't. Maybe someday I'll be able to."

"Oh," Nate said.

"Weird present, huh? I couldn't think of anything else."

"You *are* weird," Nate said with a short laugh. He took a breath, deep and shuddery. "Night."

"Night."

# 9. A Family Secret

I've always loved to watch Mom and Dad laugh. I mean really laugh, those sudden fits of belly laughter that sneak up hard and sudden and cramp them over and leave them red-faced and gasping like they're in pain, silent for a few seconds, before they start howling away like baboons. When they laugh like that it's as though my bones get filled with a new kind of air: I feel light as a bird, like if I don't grab onto something heavy—a chair or a table—I just might float off into the sky.

Two days after Christmas we came home from Vermont. Dad started telling jokes during the long drive back, and I actually saw Mom smile a couple times. Dad, too. Once I even heard a kind of snort or chuckle come out of his mouth. But I really missed the sound of their deep belly laughs. It was a sound I wasn't at all sure I'd ever hear again.

Back home life tried to go back to normal, even though it couldn't. Things would never be the same. Teddy might outgrow his wild streak, and Cyn might outgrow thinking she was a member of the Wynn family, but I knew I'd never outgrow Brad's death.

It still bothered me that I couldn't cry about Brad. My own name, Cliff, seemed to have taken on a new meaning: I felt as if I had walked to the edge of the cliff inside me, but for some reason I couldn't step over the edge.

The second night home from Vermont I dreamed about Brad. We were walking in a sunny field. It seemed like late summer in the dream. Brad was showing me how grass spiders would run ahead of your feet if you kicked the grass in a special way.

"Watch," he said. He kicked, and I saw the spiders flash, like sparks, at his toes. The dream was strange and beautiful. The spiders sparked from his feet while Brad walked along and grinned up at me, barefoot and unafraid. The dream felt so real I wanted it to go on and on forever.

I woke up with my heart beating hard, and I had the feeling that I'd just spent time with Brad, not dream time but real time. I opened my eyes. The bedroom was empty, and all at once I realized I was crying. But that was all right. In a strange way it felt all right to be crying, as though I was finally getting down to eating that bowl of sadness Uncle Billy talked about.

Aunt Pat called to see if we were coming to their house for the big holiday party they held every year. I figured for sure we'd skip it this year, but the next morning a big box of figs arrived on the UPS truck, and that afternoon Dad started to cook. I could hear him in the kitchen dragging out mixer and bowls, eggs and molasses, nutmeg and cinnamon, buttermilk and lemon. A little while later he came out of the kitchen into the TV room.

"I'm making fig pudding," he said. "Anybody want to help?"

We all looked up at him. That was the first time he'd ever wanted anyone to help him in the kitchen. I didn't know what to say.

"I could use a little help," Dad said.

"You're telling me," Nate muttered.

"Admit it, you love my fig pudding," Dad said, frowning at Nate. "How about it? Any volunteers? Cyn? Teddy?"

Nate, Teddy, and I all pitched in, and four hours later it was finished: a huge bowl of brownish, disgusting-looking goop.

"I won't say what it looks like," Nate said.

"Don't," Dad told him. "But don't worry—it always tastes ten times better than it looks."

Next morning, after breakfast, we got ready. Getting

dressed up was the only bad thing about the holiday feast at Aunt Pat and Uncle Arthur's house. Mom made us put on "church clothes"—which most of us hated, but she wouldn't budge. When everybody was ready, Dad poured the fig pudding into a big fancy bowl and covered it with clear plastic wrap. We got into the car, and the last thing Dad did before getting in was to set the bowl of fig pudding carefully on the floor of the car, right in front of me.

It took a little over an hour to get to Aunt Pat's house. There were so many cars parked in front we had to park way down the street, two blocks away.

"Remember, everyone: good manners!" Mom said. She turned around and looked hard at Teddy.

Doors opened; Teddy and Josh were eager to get out of the car. Josh lurched past me and, before I could stop him, stepped right into the fig pudding! His whole foot broke through the plastic wrap and sunk deep down into the brownish pudding, way up past his ankle. He froze, turned, and gave me a sheepish look.

"Oops," he said.

Mom flipped.

"Oh, no!" she cried. "No no no no no!"

"Oh-oh," Josh said. He bit his thumb.

"How could you let that happen?" Mom said. I was surprised to find that she was talking to me.

"Me?" I said. "I, well—"

"It's all right, no big deal, don't worry," Dad said. He knelt down to pull Josh's leg out. It wouldn't budge.

"Stuck," Josh said.

"Hold the bowl down," Dad told me.

Dad pulled again on Josh's leg, harder this time, and we heard a loud sucking sound before his foot and leg finally came free. The sweet figgy smell of the pudding filled the car. Josh stood on the sidewalk, wearing one good shoe on one foot and nothing but a sock on the other.

"My shoe's stuck!" Josh pointed at the pudding.

"HIS SHOE!" Teddy screamed.

"I can't believe this!" Mom put her hands to her face and turned around so she didn't have to look. "I cannot believe this!"

"I CAN GET IT OUT!" Teddy shouted. "LEMME TRY!"

"Stand back!" Dad said. "There's enough of a mess already! No sense anyone else getting dirty."

He rolled up his sleeve, reached into the fig pudding, and pulled out the shoe. He held it carefully, thickly clotted with pudding, away from his body. I tried not to giggle. Dad put Josh's shoe on the sidewalk.

"Disgusting!" Cyn cried. Nate reached over and used one finger to take a little of the pudding off the front of the shoe.

"Stop that!" Mom gave him a sharp look.

Dad got a roll of paper towels out of the trunk and started cleaning off his hands.

"This isn't happening," Mom said.

"Relax," Dad told her, bending down to the leg of Josh's pants. As best he could, he wiped off the sticky pudding.

"Figgy foot!" Teddy giggled, pointing at the shoe. "Figgy foot! Figgy figgy figgy foot!"

"How can I relax?" Mom demanded. "That pudding you made is totally ruined. We've got nothing to bring. We might as well get back in the car and go home."

"I wouldn't say it's ruined," Dad said. He was working on Josh's shoe, calmly cleaning it off with sheets of paper towel.

"Not ruined?" Mom said. "He *stepped* into it."

"This is a brand-new shoe," Dad said, holding it up. "Brand-new. Clean. Look: no dirt at all."

Eyes snapped wide open. Especially Mom's.

"Wait. You're not suggesting—"

"I am." Dad smiled. "I'm telling you, there's nothing wrong with that pudding. After I'm finished with this shoe I'm going to clean up Josh's sock. Then I'm going to take off the plastic wrap and smooth over the top of the pudding. Then we're going to carry it into the house."

"You're kidding, right?" Mom asked with a big smile.

"I'm dead serious."

Mom looked at us kids. "Your father has lost his marbles."

"Trust me," Dad said. "We're going to smile. We're

going to put the pudding on the table. We're going to serve it along with everything else. And no one will know the difference!"

"You're nuts," said Mom.

"I love you, too," Dad told her. "Trust me. It'll be all right. People will love it." He looked at us. "It'll be all right so long as nobody says anything. This'll be a little family secret, okay? Josh? Can I count on you? No matter what happens, don't say a word about this."

Eyes wide, smiling, he nodded.

"It's wrong to lie," Cyn said.

"We're not going to lie," Dad said. "We're just not going to mention anything about, you know, what just happened. All right?"

"I guess," Cyn said reluctantly.

"Teddy? You with me on this?"

"My lips are sealed," he said with a huge grin. "I wouldn't tell even if they tortured me with—"

"All right," Dad said. "Let's not smile *too* much or they'll think something's wrong."

"We don't have to eat it, do we?" Nate asked.

"For the record I'd just like to say that I think this is a crazy idea," Mom said. She shook her head. "A very bad idea."

"It'll be fine," Dad said. "Cliff, would you mind carrying the pudding inside?"

Aunt Pat and Uncle Arthur's house was slightly

insane, a traffic jam of relatives hugging and laughing just inside the front door. A loud clatter from the kitchen. Someone had the TV on in the living room with the volume too high. It was just past eleven in the morning, but three of my uncles—Uncle Richie, Uncle Billy, and Uncle Eddie—already had drinks in their hands. They were all laughing it up in the living room. A bunch of my younger cousins were taunting my Uncle Ed about his spaghetti dish:

"Eddie spaghetti with the meatball eyes
Put 'em in the oven and you get French fries!"

Uncle Eddie was a big man, hardly one to chase after anybody, but he pretended to get mad at their song and lurched after them, sending the little kids into great shrieks of laughter. One of my cousins chanted a variation on the song:

"Eddie spaghetti with the corncob ears,
Put 'em in the oven and you get six beers!"

Uncle Eddie roared and chased him, too.

I managed to avoid all the hugging and kissing and hustled the fig pudding down the hallway and into the dining room. There was barely an inch of the big table not covered with some sort of delicious food. Every year Aunt Pat set up a separate "sweet table" for all the pies, cakes, and cookies everyone brought. I left our fig pudding on the sweet table sitting innocently between Aunt Ruth's chocolate raspberry cake and Grandma Annie's blueberry pie.

I found Grandma sitting with some of my aunts in the den. She motioned me over.

"How's the Christmas cactus?" she asked.

"It's alive, I think," I said. "But still no blossoms. Not a single one."

"That's all right," she said. "Next year it'll blossom. You wait. Next year."

Aunt Pat wanted someone to organize a game for my little cousins. I heard her calling me and managed to escape to the quiet dimness of the basement. Mark and Peter, two cousins around my age, were down there playing pool. I hadn't seen them since Brad's funeral, and at first I didn't know what to say. But pretty soon we were all clowning around. They were good guys, and I was half tempted to tell them not to eat Dad's fig pudding, but I figured it was probably better to keep my mouth shut like Dad had told us to.

Dinner! A few years back Uncle Arthur always set up two tables for this feast, one for the adults and one for the kids. As the oldest kid, I used to get stuck with a bunch of screaming cousins, wishing I was sitting with the adults. But one year Aunt Marilyn said that this arrangement was "ageist" and discriminated against children. So now the kids and adults all jammed together around the big table. I found myself wedged between Mom and my three-year-old cousin, Melissa. When everyone got seated, Uncle Billy cleared his throat and waited for people to stop talking.

"Grandma Annie is going to say grace," he said. We all held hands and waited for Grandma to begin.

"Bless this food, O Lord," she began in a strong, clear voice. Then she stopped and spoke again, softer: "And bless those we love who are no longer with us. Especially Brad."

Silence. I could feel the tremble in Mom's hand.

"Amen," Dad said. He smiled. "Thanks, Grandma."

"Amen," Uncle Arthur said. "Let's eat!"

We feasted. And if you watched the people in my family eating, you wouldn't have imagined there was anything strange or unusual going on. Mom and Dad kept busy passing bowls and platters. They complimented Uncle Eddie on his spaghetti sauce, which was a little spicier than usual. They went wild over Uncle Arthur's she-crab bisque and Aunt Pat's sweet potato biscuits.

Teddy ate with good manners: he didn't try to lick his plate, or eat too much meat, or pull the soft center out of his bread and make dough balls the way he usually did.

But as the plates were cleared away, and everyone started eyeing the sweet table, I started getting this funny feeling in the pit of my belly. Nate sneaked a smile at me. Cyn looked down at her fingernails. Teddy caught my eye; his face looked serious, almost too serious. Mom and Dad were sitting directly across from each other but they avoided eye contact when Aunt Pat put the bowl of fig pudding onto the table.

"Ah!" Uncle Billy said. He smacked his lips.

"My favorite!" Aunt Marilyn said.

"There are so many other great desserts," Dad was saying. "I think I'm going for Grandma's blueberry pie."

"Pass down that fig pudding!" Uncle Eddie cried. "I've been dying for that pudding all week!"

The bowl got passed down. Uncle Richie passed it to Nate who passed it to Aunt Marilyn who passed it to me who passed it to Mom who passed it to Uncle Eddie. Uncle Eddie weighed two hundred sixty if he weighed a pound, and he had a tremendous appetite. Out of the corner of my eye I watched him put two large dollops of pudding into his bowl. He took a bite. I tried not to look, but I couldn't help it. Suddenly, he sat up. Looked at Dad. Took another bite.

"Say!" Uncle Eddie said to my father. "This is dee-li-cious! I mean it! The best fig pudding you ever made. Did you add some new ingredient this year?"

"Not really—" Dad began, but he stopped as Mom made a funny sound, half gulp and half choke. She put her napkin to her mouth, got up, and quickly rushed into the kitchen.

"Excuse me," Dad said, getting up to follow her.

"You really ought to try this fig pudding," Uncle Eddie was saying, digging in again. "Terrific stuff!"

"'Scuse me," I mumbled, rising and pushing back my chair.

I found Mom and Dad at the small kitchen table, leaning against each other, eyes closed, tears running down their faces. Dad's shoulders were shaking. He grabbed his gut, as if in pain. Mom was red-faced, gasping for breath.

"Some new ingredient!" Mom choked, and they both let out a howl of laughter, almost a scream, a wild animal sound that startled me as it rang out and bounced off the walls and brought the other kids in our family running into the kitchen.

"Good job, Dad!" Cyn said with a huge grin.

"Couldn't have made it without Josh!" Dad said, cracking up again, falling against Mom. And suddenly I was laughing, too. We all were, laughing hard, mouths open, roaring, barely able to stand.

"Hey, what's going on here?" a voice boomed. Uncle Eddie's big face looked down sternly at us. The very sight of him made everybody laugh even harder.

"Some new ingredient!" Dad said, still red-faced and squeezing his belly. "I can't stand it!"

Uncle Eddie had a confused look on his face.

"Everything all right?" he asked. Behind him, Grandma Annie's face appeared.

"What on earth are you all laughing at?" she demanded.

"It's just . . . so . . . funny!" Dad said, shrugging and laughing some more. Uncle Eddie walked over and punched Dad lightly on the shoulder.

"Hey, nice pudding, Clifford," he said with a big smile. That cracked up everybody again. He shrugged and left. Grandma Annie stayed behind, a bemused look on her face, watching us gasp and belly laugh, with the tears running down our faces.